The Collected
Supernatural and Weird
Fiction of
Helena P. Blavatsky

The Collected Supernatural and Weird Fiction of Helena P. Blavatsky

Ten Short Stories of the Strange and Unusual
'A Bewitched Life', 'An Unsolved Mystery',
'A Story of the Mystical', 'The Blue Lotus' and
Others

Helena P. Blavatsky

LEONAUR

The Collected
Supernatural and Weird
Fiction of
Helena P. Blavatsky
Ten Short Stories of the Strange and Unusual
'A Bewitched Life', 'An Unsolved Mystery', 'A Story of the Mystical', 'The Blue Lotus'
and Others
by Helena P. Blavatsky

FIRST EDITION

Leonaur is an imprint of Oakpast Ltd

ISBN: 978-1-78282-850-1 (hardcover)
ISBN: 978-1-78282-851-8 (softcover)

http://www.leonaur.com

Contents

A Bewitched Life

(As Narrated by a Quill Pen)

INTRODUCTION

It was a dark, chilly night in September, 1884. A heavy gloom had descended over the streets of A——, a small town on the Rhine, and was hanging like a black funeral-pall over the dull factory burgh. The greater number of its inhabitants, wearied by their long day's work, had hours before retired to stretch their tired limbs, and lay their aching heads upon their pillows. All was quiet in the large house; all was quiet in the deserted streets.

I too was lying in my bed; alas, not one of rest, but of pain and sickness, to which I had been confined for some days. So still was everything in the house, that, as Longfellow has it, its stillness seemed almost audible. I could plainly hear the murmur of the blood, as it rushed through my aching body, producing that monotonous singing so familiar to one who lends a watchful ear to silence. I had listened to it until, in my nervous imagination, it had grown into the sound of a distant cataract, the fall of mighty waters ... when, suddenly changing its character, the ever growing "singing" merged into other and far more welcome sounds. It was the low, and at first scarce audible, whisper of a human voice.

It approached, and gradually strengthening seemed to speak in my very ear. Thus sounds a voice speaking across a blue quiescent lake, in one of those wondrously acoustic gorges of the snow-capped mountains, where the air is so pure that a word pronounced half a mile off seems almost at the elbow. Yes; it was the voice of one whom to know is to reverence; of one, to me, owing to many mystic associations, most dear and holy; a voice familiar for long years and ever welcome: doubly so in hours of mental or physical suffering, for it always brings with it a ray of hope and consolation.

It whispered in gentle, mellow tones:

Courage. Think of the days passed by you in sweet associations; of the great lessons received of Nature's truths; of the many errors of men concerning these truths; and try to add to them the experience of a night in this city. Let the narrative of a strange life, that will interest you, help to shorten the hours of suffering. . . . Give your attention. Look yonder before you!

"Yonder" meant the clear, large windows of an empty house on the other side of the narrow street of the German town. They faced my own in almost a straight line across the street, and my bed faced the windows of my sleeping room. Obedient to the suggestion, I directed my gaze towards them, and what I saw made me for the time being forget the agony of the pain that racked my swollen arm and rheumatical body.

Over the windows was creeping a mist; a dense, heavy, serpentine, whitish mist, that looked like the huge shadow of a gigantic boa slowly uncoiling its body. Gradually it disappeared, to leave a lustrous light, soft and silvery, as though the window-panes behind reflected a thousand moonbeams, a tropical star-lit sky—first from outside, then from within the empty rooms. Next I saw the mist elongating itself and throwing, as it were, a fairy bridge across the street from the bewitched windows to my own balcony, nay to my very own bed. As I continued gazing, the wall and windows and the opposite house itself, suddenly vanished.

The space occupied by the empty rooms had changed into the interior of another smaller room, in what I knew to be a Swiss *châlet*—into a study, whose old, dark walls were covered from floor to ceiling with book shelves on which were many antiquated folios, as well as works of a more recent date. In the centre stood a large old-fashioned table, littered over with manuscripts and writing materials. Before it, quill-pen in hand, sat an old man; a grim-looking, skeleton-like personage, with a face so thin, so pale, yellow and emaciated, that the light of the solitary little student's lamp was reflected in two shining spots on his high cheek-bones, as though they were carved out of ivory.

As I tried to get a better view of him by slowly raising myself upon my pillows, the whole vision, *châlet* and study, desk, books and scribe, seemed to flicker and move. Once set in motion they approached nearer and nearer, until, gliding noiselessly along the fleecy bridge of clouds across the street, they floated through the closed windows into my room and finally seemed to settle beside my bed.

"Listen to what he thinks and is going to write"—said in soothing tones the same familiar, far off, and yet near voice. "Thus you will hear a narrative, the telling of which may help to shorten the long sleepless hours, and even make you forget for a while your pain. . . . Try!"—it added, using the well-known Rosicrucian and Kabalistic formula.

I tried, doing as I was bid. I centred all my attention on the solitary laborious figure that I saw before me, but which did not see me. At first, the noise of the quill-pen with which the old man was writing, suggested to my mind nothing more than a low whispered murmur of a nondescript nature. Then, gradually, my ear caught the indistinct words of a faint and distant voice, and I thought the figure before me, bending over its manuscript, was reading its tale aloud instead of writing it. But I soon found out my error. For casting my gaze at the old scribe's face, I saw at a glance that his lips were compressed and motionless, and the voice too thin and shrill to be his voice.

Stranger still, at every word traced by the feeble, aged hand, I noticed a light flashing from under his pen, a bright coloured spark that became instantaneously a sound, or—what is the same thing—it seemed to do so to my inner perceptions. It was indeed the small voice of the quill that I heard, though scribe

9

"I NOTICED A LIGHT FLASHING FROM UNDER HIS PEN, A BRIGHT
COLOURED SPARK THAT BECAME INSTANTANEOUSLY A SOUND. IT
WAS THE SMALL VOICE OF THE QUILL."

and pen were at the time, perchance, hundreds of miles away from Germany. Such things will happen occasionally, especially at night, beneath whose starry shade, as Byron tells us, we:

. . . learn the language of another world . . .

However it may be, the words uttered by the quill remained in my memory for days after. Nor had I any great difficulty in retaining them, for when I sat down to record the story, I found it, as usual, indelibly impressed on the astral tablets before my inner eye.

Thus, I had but to copy it and so give it as I received it. I failed to learn the name of the unknown nocturnal writer. Nevertheless, though the reader may prefer to regard the whole story as one made up for the occasion, a dream, perhaps, still its incidents will, I hope, prove none the less interesting.

1: THE STRANGER'S STORY

My birthplace is a small mountain hamlet, a cluster of Swiss cottages, hidden deep in a sunny nook, between two tumble-down glaciers and a peak covered with eternal snows. Thither, thirty-seven years ago, I returned—crippled mentally and physically—to die, if death would only have me. The pure invigorating air of my birthplace decided otherwise. I am still alive; perhaps for the purpose of giving evidence to facts I have kept profoundly secret from all—a tale of horror I would rather hide than reveal. The reason for this unwillingness on my part is due to my early education, and to subsequent events that gave the lie to my most cherished prejudices. Some people might be inclined to regard these events as providential: I, however, believe in no Providence, and yet am unable to attribute them to mere chance. I connect them as the ceaseless evolution of effects, engendered by certain direct causes, with one primary and fundamental cause, from which ensued all that followed.

A feeble old man am I now, yet physical weakness has in no way impaired my mental faculties. I remember the smallest details of that terrible cause, which engendered such fatal results. It is these which furnish me with an additional proof of the

11

actual existence of one whom I fain would regard—oh, that I could do so!—as a creature born of my fancy, the evanescent production of a feverish, horrid dream! Oh that terrible, mild and all-forgiving, that saintly and respected Being! It was that paragon of all the virtues who embittered my whole existence. It is he, who, pushing me violently out of the monotonous but secure groove of daily life, was the first to force upon me the certitude of a life hereafter, thus adding an additional horror to one already great enough.

With a view to a clearer comprehension of the situation, I must interrupt these recollections with a few words about myself. Oh how, if I could, would I obliterate that hated *Self!*

Born in Switzerland, of French parents, who centred the whole world-wisdom in the literary trinity of Voltaire, J. J. Rousseau and D'Holbach, and educated in a German university, I grew up a thorough materialist, a confirmed atheist. I could never have even pictured to myself any beings—least of all a Being—above or even outside visible nature, as distinguished from her. Hence I regarded everything that could not be brought under the strictest analysis of the physical senses as a mere chimera. A soul, I argued, even supposing man has one, must be material. According to Origen's definition, *incorporeus* (**ἀσώματος.**)— the epithet he gave to his God—signifies a substance only more subtle than that of physical bodies, of which, at best, we can form no definite idea. How then can that, of which our senses cannot enable us to obtain any clear knowledge, how can that make itself visible or produce any tangible manifestations?

Accordingly, I received the tales of nascent Spiritualism with a feeling of utter contempt, and regarded the overtures made by certain priests with derision, often akin to anger. And indeed the latter feeling has never entirely abandoned me.

Pascal, in the eighth Act of his *Thoughts*, confesses to a most complete incertitude upon the existence of God. Throughout my life, I too professed a complete certitude as to the non-existence of any such extra-cosmic being, and repeated with that great thinker the memorable words in which he tells us:

I have examined if this God of whom all the world speaks might not have left some marks of himself. I look everywhere, and everywhere I see nothing but obscurity. Nature offers me nothing that may not be a matter of doubt and inquietude.

Nor have I found to this day anything that might unsettle me in precisely similar and even stronger feelings. I have never believed, nor shall I ever believe, in a Supreme Being. But at the potentialities of man, proclaimed far and wide in the East, powers so developed in some persons as to make them virtually Gods, at them I laugh no more. My whole broken life is a protest against such negation. I believe in such phenomena, and—I curse them, whenever they come, and by whatsoever means generated.

On the death of my parents, owing to an unfortunate lawsuit, I lost the greater part of my fortune, and resolved—for the sake of those I loved best, rather than for my own—to make another for myself. My elder sister, whom I adored, had married a poor man. I accepted the offer of a rich Hamburg firm and sailed for Japan as its junior partner.

For several years my business went on successfully. I got into the confidence of many influential Japanese, through whose protection I was enabled to travel and transact business in many localities, which, in those days especially, were not easily accessible to foreigners. Indifferent to every religion, I became interested in the philosophy of Buddhism, the only religious system I thought worthy of being called philosophical. Thus, in my moments of leisure, I visited the most remarkable temples of Japan, the most important and curious of the ninety-six Buddhist monasteries of Kioto. I have examined in turn Day-Bootzoo, with its gigantic bell; Tzeonene, Enarino-Yassero, Kie-Missoo, Higadzi-Hong-Vonsi, and many other famous temples.

Several years passed away, and during that whole period I was not cured of my scepticism, nor did I ever contemplate having my opinions on this subject altered. I derided the pretentions of the Japanese bonzes and ascetics, as I had those of Christian priests and European Spiritualists. I could not believe in the acquisition of powers unknown to, and never studied by, men of science; hence I scoffed at all such ideas. The superstitious and atrabilious Buddhist, teaching us to shun the pleasures of life, to put to rout one's passions, to render oneself insensible alike to happiness and suffering, in order to acquire such chimerical powers—seemed supremely ridiculous in my eyes.

On a day for ever memorable to me—a fatal day—I made the acquaintance of a venerable and learned Bonze, a Japanese priest, named Tamoora Hideyeri. I met him at the foot of the golden Kwon-On, and from that moment he became my best and most trusted friend. Notwithstanding my great and genuine regard for him, however, whenever a good opportunity was offered I never failed to mock his religious convictions, thereby very often hurting his feelings.

But my old friend was as meek and forgiving as any true Buddhist's heart might desire. He never resented my impatient sarcasms, even when they were, to say the least, of equivocal propriety, and generally limited his replies to the "wait and see" kind of protest. Nor could he be brought to seriously believe in the sincerity of my denial of the existence of any God or Gods. The full meaning of the terms "atheism" and "scepticism" was beyond the comprehension of his otherwise extremely intellectual and acute mind. Like certain reverential Christians, he seemed incapable of realising that any man of sense should prefer the wise conclusions arrived at by philosophy and modern science to a ridiculous belief in an invisible world full of Gods and spirits, *dzins* and demons.

"Man is a spiritual being," he insisted, "who returns to earth more than once, and is rewarded or punished in the between times." The proposition that man is nothing else but a heap of organized dust, was beyond him. Like Jeremy Collier, he refused to admit that he was no better than "a stalking machine, a speaking head without a soul in it," whose "thoughts are all bound by the laws of motion."

"For," he argued, "if my actions were, as you say, prescribed beforehand, and I had no more liberty or free will to change the course of my action than the running waters of the river yonder, then the glorious doctrine of Karma, of merit and demerit, would be foolishness indeed."

Thus the whole of my hyper-metaphysical friend's ontology rested on the shaky superstructure of metempsychosis, of a fancied "just" Law of Retribution, and other such equally absurd dreams.

"We cannot," said he paradoxically one day, "hope to live hereafter in the full enjoyment of our consciousness, unless we have built for it beforehand a firm and solid foundation of spirituality. . . . Nay, laugh not, friend of no faith," he meekly pleaded, "but rather think and reflect on this. One who has never taught himself to live in Spirit during his conscious and responsible life on earth, can hardly hope to enjoy a sentient existence after death, when, deprived of his body, he is limited to that Spirit alone."

"What can you mean by life in Spirit?"—I inquired.

"Life on a spiritual plane; that which the Buddhists call *Tushita Devaloka* (Paradise). Man can create such a blissful existence for himself between two births, by the gradual transference on to that plane of all the faculties which during his sojourn on earth manifest through his organic body and, as you call it, animal brain.". . .

"How absurd! And how can man do this?"

"Contemplation and a strong desire to assimilate the blessed Gods, will enable him to do so."

"And if man refuses this intellectual occupation, by which you mean, I suppose, the fixing of the eyes on the tip of his nose, what becomes of him after the death of his body?" was my mocking question.

"He will be dealt with according to the prevailing state of his consciousness, of which there are many grades. At best—immediate rebirth; at worst—the state of *avitchi*, a mental hell. Yet one need not be an ascetic to assimilate spiritual life which will extend to the hereafter. All that is required is to try to approach

Spirit."

"How so? Even when disbelieving in it?"—I rejoined.

"Even so! One may disbelieve and yet harbour in one's nature room for doubt, however small that room may be, and thus try one day, were it but for one moment, to open the door of the inner temple; and this will prove sufficient for the purpose."

"You are decidedly poetical, and paradoxical to boot, reverend sir. Will you kindly explain to me a little more of the mystery?"

"There is none; still I am willing. Suppose for a moment that some unknown temple to which you have never been before, and the existence of which you think you have reasons to deny, is the 'spiritual plane' of which I am speaking. Someone takes you by the hand and leads you towards its entrance, curiosity makes you open its door and look within. By this simple act, by entering it for one second, you have established an everlasting connexion between your consciousness and the temple. You cannot deny its existence any longer, nor obliterate the fact of your having entered it. And according to the character and the variety of your work, within its holy precincts, so will you live in it after your consciousness is severed from its dwelling of flesh."

"What do you mean? And what has my after-death consciousness—if such a thing exists—to do with the temple?"

"It has everything to do with it," solemnly rejoined the old man. "There can be no self-consciousness after death outside the temple of spirit. That which you will have done within its plane will alone survive. All the rest is false and an illusion. It is doomed to perish in the Ocean of Mâyâ."

Amused at the idea of living outside one's body, I urged on my old friend to tell me more. Mistaking my meaning, the venerable man willingly consented.

Tamoora Hideyeri belonged to the great temple of Tzi-Onene, a Buddhist monastery, famous not only in all Japan, but also throughout Tibet and China. No other is so venerated in Kioto. Its monks belong to the sect of Dzeno-doo, and are considered as the most learned among the many erudite fraternities. They are, moreover, closely connected and allied with the *Yamabooshi* (the ascetics, or hermits), who follow the doctrines of Lao-tze. No wonder, that at the slightest provocation on my part the priest flew into the highest metaphysics, hoping thereby to cure me of my infidelity.

No use repeating here the long rigmarole of the most hopelessly involved and incomprehensible of all doctrines. According to his ideas, we have to train ourselves for spirituality in another world—as for gymnastics. Carrying on the analogy between the temple and the "spiritual plane" he tried to illustrate his idea. He had himself worked in the temple of Spirit two-thirds of his life, and given several hours daily to "contemplation." Thus *he knew*(?!) that after he had laid aside his mortal casket, "a mere illusion," he explained—he would in his spiritual consciousness live over again every feeling of ennobling joy and divine bliss he had ever had, or *ought to have had*—only a hundred-fold intensified. His work on the spirit-plane had been considerable, he said, and he hoped, therefore, that the wages of the laborer would prove proportionate.

"But suppose the laborer, as in the example you have just brought forward in my case, should have no more than opened the temple door out of mere curiosity; had only peeped into the sanctuary never to set his foot therein again. What then?"

"Then," he answered, "you would have only this short minute to record in your future self-consciousness and no more. Our life hereafter records and repeats but the impressions and feelings we have had in our spiritual experiences and nothing else. Thus, if instead of reverence at the moment of entering the abode of Spirit, you had been harbouring in your heart anger, jealousy or grief, then your future spiritual life would be a sad one, in truth. There would be nothing to record, save the opening of a door in a fit of bad temper."

"How then could it be repeated?"—I insisted, highly amused. "What do you suppose I would be doing before incarnating again?"

"In that case," he said, speaking slowly and weighing every

word—"in that case, *you would have, I fear, only to open and shut the temple door, over and over again, during a period which, however short, would seem to you an eternity.*"

This kind of after-death occupation appeared to me, at that time, so grotesque in its sublime absurdity, that I was seized with an almost inextinguishable fit of laughter.

My venerable friend looked considerably dismayed at such a result of his metaphysical instruction. He had evidently not expected such hilarity. However, he said nothing, but only sighed and gazed at me with increased benevolence and pity shining in his small black eyes.

"Pray excuse my laughter," I apologised. "But really, now, you cannot seriously mean to tell me that the 'spiritual state' you advocate and so firmly believe in, consists only in aping certain things we do in life?"

"Nay, nay; not aping, but only intensifying their repetition; filling the gaps that were unjustly left unfilled during life in the fruition of our acts and deeds, and of everything performed on the spiritual plane of the one real state. What I said was an illustration, and no doubt for you, who seem entirely ignorant of the mysteries of *Soul-Vision*, not a very intelligible one. It is myself who am to be blamed. . . What I sought to impress upon you was that, as the spiritual state of our consciousness liberated from its body is but the fruition of every spiritual act performed during life, where an act had been barren, there could be no results expected—save the repetition of that act itself. This is all. I pray you may be spared such fruitless deeds and finally made to see certain truths." And passing through the usual Japanese courtesies of taking leave, the excellent man departed.

Alas, alas! had I but known at the time what I have learned since, how little would I have laughed, and how much more would I have learned!

But as the matter stood, the more personal affection and respect I felt for him, the less could I become reconciled to his wild ideas about an after-life, and especially as to the acquisition by some men of supernatural powers. I felt particularly disgusted

with his reverence for the *Yamabooshi*, the allies of every Buddhist sect in the land. Their claims to the "miraculous" were
simply odious to my notions. To hear every Jap I knew at Kioto,
even to my own partner, the shrewdest of all the business men
I had come across in the East—mentioning these followers of
Lao-tze with downcast eyes, reverentially folded hands, and affirmations of their possessing "great" and "wonderful" gifts, was
more than I was prepared to patiently tolerate in those days.

And who were they, after all, these great magicians with their
ridiculous pretensions to super-mundane knowledge; these
"holy beggars" who, as I then thought, purposely dwell in the
recesses of unfrequented mountains and on unapproachable
craggy steeps, so as the better to afford no chance to curious
intruders of finding them out and watching them in their own
dens? Simply impudent fortune-tellers, Japanese gypsies who
sell charms and talismans, and no better. In answer to those who
sought to assure me that though the *Yamabooshi* lead a mysterious life, admitting none of the profane to their secrets, they still
do accept pupils, however difficult it is for one to become their
disciple, and that thus they have living witnesses to the great
purity and sanctity of their lives, in answer to such affirmations I
opposed the strongest negation and stood firmly by it.

I insulted both masters and pupils, classing them under the
same category of fools, when not knaves, and I went so far as
to include in this number the Sintos. Now Sintoism or *Sin-Syu*,
"faith in the Gods, and in the way to the Gods," that is, belief in
the communication between these creatures and men, is a kind
of worship of nature-spirits, than which nothing can be more
miserably absurd. And by placing the Sintos among the fools
and knaves of other sects, I gained many enemies. For the Sinto
Kanusi (spiritual teachers) are looked upon as the highest in the
upper classes of Society, the Mikado himself being at the head
of their hierarchy and the members of the sect belonging to the
most cultured and educated men in Japan. These Kanusi of the
Sinto form no caste or class apart, nor do they pass any ordina-
tion—at any rate none known to outsiders.

And as they claim publicly no special privilege or powers, even their dress being in no wise different from that of the laity, but are simply in the world's opinion professors and students of occult and spiritual sciences, I very often came in contact with them without in the least suspecting that I was in the presence of such personages.

2: THE MYSTERIOUS VISITOR

Years passed; and as time went by, my ineradicable scepticism grew stronger and waxed fiercer every day. I have already mentioned an elder and much-beloved sister, my only surviving relative. She had married and had lately gone to live at Nuremberg. I regarded her with feelings more filial than fraternal, and her children were as dear to me as might have been my own. At the time of the great catastrophe that in the course of a few days had made my father lose his large fortune, and my mother break her heart, she it was, that sweet big sister of mine, who had made herself of her own accord the guardian angel of our ruined family.

Out of her great love for me, her younger brother, for whom she attempted to replace the professors that could no longer be afforded, she had renounced her own happiness. She sacrificed herself and the man she loved, by indefinitely postponing their marriage, in order to help our father and chiefly myself by her undivided devotion. And, oh, how I loved and reverenced her, time but strengthening this earliest family affection! They who maintain that no atheist, as such, can be a true friend, an affectionate relative, or a loyal subject, utter—whether consciously or unconsciously—the greatest calumny and lie. To say that a materialist grows hard-hearted as he grows older, that he cannot love as a believer does, is simply the greatest fallacy.

There may be such exceptional cases it is true, but these are found only occasionally in men who are even more selfish than they are sceptical, or vulgarly worldly. But when a man who is kindly disposed in his nature, for no selfish motives but because of reason and love of truth, becomes what is called atheistical, he

20

is only strengthened in his family affections, and in his sympathies with his fellow men. All his emotions, all the ardent aspirations towards the unseen and unreachable, all the love which he would otherwise have uselessly bestowed on a suppositional heaven and its God, become now centred with tenfold force upon his loved ones and mankind. Indeed, the atheist's heart alone—

> . . . *can know,*
> *What secret tides of still enjoyment flow*
> *When brothers love*

It was such holy fraternal love that led me also to sacrifice my comfort and personal welfare to secure her happiness, the felicity of her who had been more than a mother to me. I was a mere youth when I left home for Hamburg. There, working with all the desperate earnestness of a man who has but one noble object in view—to relieve suffering, and help those whom he loves—I very soon secured the confidence of my employers, who raised me in consequence to the high post of trust I always enjoyed. My first real pleasure and reward in life was to see my sister married to the man she had sacrificed for my sake, and to help them in their struggle for existence. So purifying and unselfish was this affection of mine for her that when it came to be shared among her children, instead of losing in intensity by such division, it seemed only to grow the stronger.

Born with the potentiality of the warmest family affection in me, the devotion for my sister was so great, that the thought of burning that sacred fire of love before any idol, save that of herself and family, never entered my head. This was the only church I recognised, the only church wherein I worshipped at the altar of holy family affection. In fact this large family of eleven persons, including her husband, was the only tie that attached me to Europe. Twice during a period of nine years, had I crossed the ocean with the sole object of seeing and pressing these dear ones to my heart. I had no other business in the West; and having performed this pleasant duty, I returned each time to Japan to work and toil for them. For their sake I remained a bachelor, that the wealth I might acquire should go undivided to them alone.

We had always corresponded as regularly as the long transit of the then very irregular service of the mail-boats would permit. But suddenly there came a break in my letters from home. For nearly a year I received no intelligence; and day by day, I became more restless, more apprehensive of some great misfortune. Vainly I looked for a letter, a simple message; and my efforts to account for so unusual a silence were fruitless.

"Friend," said to me one day Tamoora Hideyeri, my only confidant, "Friend, consult a holy *Yamabooshi* and you will feel at rest."

Of course the offer was rejected with as much moderation as I could command under the provocation. But, as steamer after steamer came in without a word of news, I felt a despair which daily increased in depth and fixity. This finally degenerated into an irrepressible craving, a morbid desire to learn—the worst as I then thought. I struggled hard with the feeling, but it had the best of me. Only a few months before a complete master of myself—I now became an abject slave to fear. A fatalist of the school of D'Holbach, I, who had always regarded belief in the system of necessity as being the only promoter of philosophical happiness, and as having the most advantageous influence over human weaknesses, *I* felt a craving for something akin to fortune-telling!

I had gone so far as to forget the first principle of my doctrine—the only one calculated to calm our sorrows, to inspire us with a useful submission, namely a rational resignation to the decrees of blind destiny, with which foolish sensibility causes us so often to be overwhelmed—the doctrine that *all is necessary*. Yes; forgetting this, I was drawn into a shameful, superstitious longing, a stupid, disgraceful desire to learn—if not futurity, at any rate that which was taking place at the other side of the globe.

My conduct seemed utterly modified, my temperament and aspirations wholly changed; and like a weak, nervous girl,

I caught myself straining my mind to the very verge of lunacy in an attempt to look—as I had been told one could sometimes do—beyond the oceans, and learn, at last, the real cause of this long, inexplicable silence!

One evening, at sunset, my old friend, the venerable Bonze, Tamoora, appeared on the verandah of my low wooden house. I had not visited him for many days, and he had come to know how I was. I took the opportunity to once more sneer at one, whom, in reality, I regarded with most affectionate respect. With equivocal taste—for which I repented almost before the words had been pronounced—I inquired of him why he had taken the trouble to walk all that distance when he might have learned anything he liked about me by simply interrogating a *Yamabooshi*? He seemed a little hurt, at first; but after keenly scrutinising my dejected face, he mildly remarked that he could only insist upon what he had advised before. Only one of that holy order could give me consolation in my present state.

From that instant, an insane desire possessed me to challenge him to prove his assertions. I defied—I said to him—any and every one of his alleged magicians to tell me the name of the person I was thinking of, and what he was doing at that moment. He quietly answered that my desire could be easily satisfied. There was a *Yamabooshi* two doors from me, visiting a sick Sinto. He would fetch him—if I only said the word.

I said it and *from the moment of its utterance my doom was sealed.*

How shall I find words to describe the scene that followed! Twenty minutes after the desire had been so incautiously expressed, an old Japanese, uncommonly tall and majestic for one of that race, pale, thin and emaciated, was standing before me. There, where I had expected to find servile obsequiousness, I only discerned an air of calm and dignified composure, the attitude of one who knows his moral superiority, and therefore scorns to notice the mistakes of those who fail to recognise it. To the somewhat irreverent and mocking questions, which I put to him one after another, with feverish eagerness, he made no reply; but gazed on me in silence as a physician would look at a delirious patient.

From the moment he fixed his eye on mine, I felt—or shall I say, saw—as though it were a sharp ray of light, a thin silvery thread, shoot out from the intensely black and narrow eyes so deeply sunk in the yellow old face. It seemed to penetrate into my brain and heart like an arrow, and set to work to dig out therefrom every thought and feeling. Yes; I both saw and felt it, and very soon the double sensation became intolerable.

To break the spell I defied him to tell me what he had found in my thoughts. Calmly came the correct answer—Extreme anxiety for a female relative, her husband and children, who were inhabiting a house the correct description of which he gave as though he knew it as well as myself. I turned a suspicious eye upon my friend, the Bonze, to whose indiscretions, I thought, I was indebted for the quick reply.

Remembering however that Tamoora could know nothing of the appearance of my sister's house, that the Japanese are proverbially truthful and, as friends, faithful to death—I felt ashamed of my suspicion.

To atone for it before my own conscience I asked the hermit whether he could tell me anything of the present state of that beloved sister of mine. The foreigner—was the reply—would never believe in the words, or trust to the knowledge of any person but himself. Were the *Yamabooshi* to tell him, the impression would wear out hardly a few hours later, and the inquirer find himself as miserable as before.

There was but one means; and that was to make the foreigner (myself) see with his own eyes, and thus learn the truth for himself. Was the inquirer ready to be placed by a *Yamabooshi*, a stranger to him, in the required state?

I had heard in Europe of mesmerized somnambules and pretenders to clairvoyance, and having no faith in them, I had, therefore, nothing against the process itself. Even in the midst of my never-ceasing mental agony, I could not help smiling at the ridiculous nature of the operation I was willingly submitting to. Nevertheless I silently bowed consent.

3: PSYCHIC MAGIC

The old *Yamabooshi* lost no time. He looked at the setting sun, and finding probably, the Lord Ten-Dzio-Dai-Dzio (the Spirit who darts his Rays) propitious for the coming ceremony, he speedily drew out a little bundle. It contained a small lacquered box, a piece of vegetable paper, made from the bark of the mulberry tree, and a pen, with which he traced upon the paper a few sentences in the *Naiden* character—a peculiar style of written language used only for religious and mystical purposes. Having finished, he exhibited from under his clothes a small round mirror of steel of extraordinary brilliancy, and placing it before my eyes, asked me to look into it.

I had not only heard before of these mirrors, which are frequently used in the temples, but I had often seen them. It is claimed that under the direction and will of instructed priests, there appear in them the Daij-Dzin, the great spirits who notify the inquiring devotees of their fate. I first imagined that his intention was to evoke such a spirit, who would answer my queries. What happened, however, was something of quite a different character.

No sooner had I, not without a last pang of mental squeamishness, produced by a deep sense of my own absurd position, touched the mirror, than I suddenly felt a strange sensation in the arm of the hand that held it. For a brief moment I forgot to "sit in the seat of the scorner" and failed to look at the matter from a ludicrous point of view. Was it fear that suddenly clutched my brain, for an instant paralysing its activity—

. . . that fear
When the heart longs to know, what it is death to hear?

No; for I still had consciousness enough left to go on persuading myself that nothing would come out of an experiment, in the nature of which no sane man could ever believe. What was it then, that crept across my brain like a living thing of ice, producing therein a sensation of horror, and then clutched at my heart as if a deadly serpent had fastened its fangs into it? With a convulsive jerk of the hand I dropped the—I blush to write the adjective—"magic" mirror, and could not force myself to pick it up from the settee on which I was reclining. For one short moment there was a terrible struggle between some undefined, and to me utterly inexplicable, longing to look into the depths of the polished surface of the mirror and my pride, the ferocity of which nothing seemed capable of taming.

It was finally so tamed, however, its revolt being conquered by its own defiant intensity. There was an opened novel lying on a lacquer table near the settee, and as my eyes happened to fall upon its pages, I read the words, "*The veil which covers futurity is woven by the hand of mercy.*" This was enough. That same pride which had hitherto held me back from what I regarded as a degrading, superstitious experiment, caused me to challenge my fate. I picked up the ominously shining disk and prepared to look into it.

While I was examining the mirror, the *Yamabooshi* hastily spoke a few words to the Bonze, Tamoora, at which I threw a furtive and suspicious glance at both. I was wrong once more.

"The holy man desires me to put you a question and give you at the same time a warning," remarked the Bonze. "If you are willing to see for yourself now, you will have—under the penalty of *seeing for ever, in the hereafter, all that is taking place, at whatever distance, and that against your will or inclination*—to submit to a regular course of purification, after you have learned what you want through the mirror."

"What is this course, and what have I to promise?" I asked defiantly.

"It is for your own good. You must promise him to submit to the process, lest, for the rest of his life, he should have to hold himself responsible, before his own conscience, for having made an *irresponsible* seer of you. Will you do so, friend?"

"There will be time enough to think of it, if I see anything"— I sneeringly replied, adding under my breath—"something I doubt a good deal, so far."

"Well, you are warned, friend. The consequences will now

remain with yourself," was the solemn answer.

I glanced at the clock, and made a gesture of impatience, which was remarked and understood by the *Yamabooshi*. It was just *seven minutes after five*.

"Define well in your mind *what* you would see and learn," said the "conjuror," placing the mirror and paper in my hands, and instructing me how to use them.

His instructions were received by me with more impatience than gratitude; and for one short instant, I hesitated again. Nevertheless I replied, while fixing the mirror:

"*I desire but one thing—to learn the reason or reasons why my sister has so suddenly ceased writing to me.*". . .

Had I pronounced these words in reality, and in the hearing of the two witnesses, or had I only thought them? To this day I cannot decide the point. I now remember but one thing distinctly: while I sat gazing in the mirror, the *Yamabooshi* kept gazing at me. But whether this process lasted half a second or three hours, I have never since been able to settle in my mind with any degree of satisfaction. I can recall every detail of the scene up to the moment when I took up the mirror with the left hand, holding the paper inscribed with the mystic characters between the thumb and finger of the right, when all of a sudden I seemed to quite lose consciousness of the surrounding objects.

The passage from the active waking state to one that I could compare with nothing I had ever experienced before, was so rapid, that while my eyes had ceased to perceive external objects and had completely lost sight of the Bonze, the *Yamabooshi*, and even of my room, I could nevertheless distinctly see the whole of my head and my back, as I sat leaning forward with the mirror in my hand. Then came a strong sensation of an involuntary rush forward, of *snapping* off, so to say, from my place—I had almost said from my body. And, then, while every one of my other senses had become totally paralysed, my eyes, as I thought, unexpectedly caught a clearer and far more vivid glimpse than they had ever had in reality, of my sister's new house at Nuremberg, which I had never visited and knew only from a sketch, and other scenery with which I had never been very familiar.

Together with this, and while feeling in my brain what seemed like flashes of a departing consciousness—dying persons must feel so, no doubt—the very last, vague thought, so weak as to have been hardly perceptible, was that I must look very, *very* ridiculous. . . . This *feeling*—for such it was rather than a thought—was interrupted, suddenly extinguished, so to say, by a clear *mental vision* (I cannot characterize it otherwise) of myself, of that which I regarded as, and knew to be my body, lying with ashy cheeks on the settee, dead to all intents and purposes, but still staring with the cold and glassy eyes of a corpse into the mirror. Bending over it, with his two emaciated hands cutting the air in every direction over *its* white face, stood the tall figure of the *Yamabooshi*, for whom I felt at that instant an inextinguishable, murderous hatred.

As I was going, in thought, to pounce upon the vile charlatan, my corpse, the two old men, the room itself, and every object in it, trembled and danced in a reddish glowing light, and seemed to float rapidly away from "me." A few more grotesque, distorted shadows before "my" sight; and, with a last feeling of terror and a supreme effort to realise *who then was I now, since I was not that corpse*—a great veil of darkness fell over me, like a funeral pall, and every thought in me was dead.

4: A Vision of Horror

How strange!. . . Where was I now? It was evident to me that I had once more returned to my senses. For there I was, vividly realising that I was rapidly moving forward, while experiencing a queer, strange sensation as though I were swimming, without impulse or effort on my part, and in total darkness. The idea that first presented itself to me was that of a long subterranean passage of water, of earth, and stifling air, though bodily I had no perception, no sensation, of the presence or contact of any of these. I tried to utter a few words, to repeat my last sentence, "I desire but one thing: to learn the reason or reasons why my sister has so suddenly ceased writing to me"—but the only words I heard out of the twenty-one, were the two, "*to learn*," and these, instead of their coming out of my own larynx, came back to me in my own voice, but entirely outside myself, near, but not in me. In short, they were pronounced by my voice, not by my lips. . . .

One more rapid, involuntary motion, one more plunge into the Cimmerian darkness of a (to me) unknown element, and I saw myself standing—actually standing—underground, as it seemed. I was compactly and thickly surrounded on all sides, above and below, right and left, with earth, and *in* the mould, and yet it weighed not, and seemed quite immaterial and transparent to *my senses*. I did not realise for one second the utter absurdity, nay, impossibility of that *seeming* fact! One second more, one short instant, and I perceived—oh, inexpressible horror, when I think of it now; for then, although I perceived, realised, and recorded facts and events far more clearly than ever I had done before, I did not seem to be touched in any other way by what I saw. Yes—I perceived a coffin at my feet. It was a plain unpretentious shell, made of deal, the last couch of the pauper, in which, notwithstanding its closed lid, I plainly saw a hideous, grinning skull, a man's skeleton, mutilated and broken in many of its parts, as though it had been taken out of some hidden chamber of the defunct Inquisition, where it had been subjected to torture. "Who can it be?"—I thought.

At this moment I heard again proceeding from afar the same voice—*my* voice . . . "*the reason or reasons why*" . . . it said; as though these words were the unbroken continuation of the same sentence of which it had just repeated the two words "to learn." It sounded near, and yet as from some incalculable distance; giving me then the idea that the long subterranean journey, the subsequent mental reflexions and discoveries, had occupied no time; had been performed during the short, almost instantaneous interval between the first and the middle words of the sentence, begun, at any rate, if not actually pronounced by myself in my room at Kioto, and which it was now finishing, in interrupted, broken phrases, like a faithful echo of my own

29

words and voice....

Forthwith, the hideous, mangled remains began assuming a form, and to me, but too familiar appearance. The broken parts joined together one to the other, the bones became covered once more with flesh, and I recognised in these disfigured remains—with some surprise, but not a trace of feeling at the sight—my sister's dead husband, my own brother-in-law, whom I had for her sake loved so truly. "How was it, and how did he come to die such a terrible death?"—I asked myself. To put oneself a query seemed, in the state in which I was, to instantly solve it. Hardly had I asked myself the question, when, as if in a panorama, I saw the retrospective picture of poor Karl's death, in all its horrid vividness, and with every thrilling detail, every one of which, however, left me then entirely and brutally indifferent.

Here he is, the dear old fellow, full of life and joy at the prospect of more lucrative employment from his principal, examining and trying in a wood-sawing factory a monster steam engine just arrived from America. He bends over, to examine more closely an inner arrangement, to tighten a screw. His clothes are caught by the teeth of the revolving wheel in full motion, and suddenly he is dragged down, doubled up, and his limbs half severed, torn off, before the workmen, unacquainted with the mechanism can stop it. He is taken out, or what remains of him, dead, mangled, a thing of horror, an unrecognisable mass of palpitating flesh and blood!

I follow the remains, wheeled as an unrecognisable heap to the hospital, hear the brutally given order that the messengers of death should stop on their way at the house of the widow and orphans. I follow them, and find the unconscious family quietly assembled together. I see my sister, the dear and beloved, and remain indifferent at the sight, only feeling highly interested in the coming scene. My heart, my feelings, even my personality, seemed to have disappeared, to have been left behind, to belong to somebody else.

There "I" stand, and witness her unprepared reception of the ghastly news. I realise clearly, without one moment's hesitation or mistake, the effect of the shock upon her, I perceive clearly, following and recording, to the minutest detail, her sensations and the inner process that takes place in her. I watch and remember, missing not one single point.

As the corpse is brought into the house for identification I hear the long agonising cry, my own name pronounced, and the dull thud of the living body falling upon the remains of the dead one. I follow with curiosity the sudden thrill and the instantaneous perturbation in her brain that follow it, and watch with attention the worm-like, precipitate, and immensely intensified motion of the tubular fibres, the instantaneous change of colour in the cephalic extremity of the nervous system, the fibrous nervous matter passing from white to bright red and then to a dark red, bluish hue.

I notice the sudden flash of a phosphorous-like, brilliant Radiance, its tremor and its sudden extinction followed by darkness—complete darkness in the region of memory—as the Radiance, comparable in its form only to a human shape, oozes out suddenly from the top of the head, expands, loses its form and scatters. And I say to myself: "This is insanity; life-long, incurable insanity, for the principle of intelligence is not paralyzed or extinguished temporarily, but has just deserted the tabernacle for ever, ejected from it by the terrible force of the sudden blow.... The link between the animal and the divine essence is broken.". .... And as the unfamiliar term "divine" is mentally uttered *my* "*thought*"—laughs.

Suddenly I hear again my far-off yet near voice pronouncing emphatically and close by me the words ... "*why my sister has so suddenly ceased writing.*"... And before the two final words "*to me*" have completed the sentence, I see a long series of sad events, immediately following the catastrophe.

I behold the mother, now a helpless, grovelling idiot, in the lunatic asylum attached to the city hospital, the seven younger children admitted into a refuge for paupers. Finally I see the two elder, a boy of fifteen, and a girl a year younger, my favourites, both taken by strangers into their service. A captain of a sailing

31

vessel carries away my nephew, an old Jewess adopts the tender girl. I see the events with all their horrors and thrilling details, and record each, to the smallest detail, with the utmost coolness.

For, mark well: when I use such expressions as "horrors," etc., they are to be understood as an afterthought. During the whole time of the events described I experienced no sensation of either pain or pity. My feelings seemed to be paralyzed as well as my external senses; it was only after "coming back" that I realised my irretrievable losses to their full extent.

Much of that which I had so vehemently denied in those days, owing to sad personal experience I have to admit now. Had I been told by anyone at that time, that man could act and think and feel, irrespective of his brain and senses; nay, that by some mysterious, and to this day, for me, incomprehensible power, *he* could be transported *mentally*, thousands of miles away from his body, there to witness not only present but also past events, and remember these by storing them in his memory—I would have proclaimed that man a madman. Alas, I can do so no longer, for I have become myself that "madman."

Ten, twenty, forty, a hundred times during the course of this wretched life of mine, have I experienced and lived over such moments of existence, *outside of my body*. Accursed be that hour when this terrible power was first awakened in me! I have not even the consolation left of attributing such glimpses of events at a distance to insanity. Madmen rave and see that which exists not in the realm they belong to. My visions have proved *invariably correct*. But to my narrative of woe.

I had hardly had time to see my unfortunate young niece in her new Israelitish home, when I felt a shock of the same nature as the one that had sent me "swimming" through the bowels of the earth, as I had thought. I opened my eyes in my own room, and the first thing I fixed upon by accident, was the clock. The hands of the dial showed seven minutes and a half past five! . . . I had thus passed through these most terrible experiences, which it takes me hours to narrate, *in precisely half a minute of time!*

But this, too, was an after-thought. For one brief instant I recollected nothing of what I had seen. The interval between the time I had glanced at the clock when taking the mirror from the *Yamabooshi's* hand and this second glance, seemed to me merged in one. I was just opening my lips to hurry on the *Yamabooshi* with his experiment, when the full remembrance of what I had just seen flashed lightning-like into my brain. Uttering a cry of horror and despair, I felt as though the whole creation were crushing me under its weight. For one moment I remained speechless, the picture of human ruin amid a world of death and desolation. My heart sank down in anguish: my doom was closed; and a hopeless gloom seemed to settle over the rest of my life for ever.

5: RETURN OF DOUBTS

Then came a reaction as sudden as my grief itself. A doubt arose in my mind, which forthwith grew into a fierce desire of denying the truth of what I had seen. A stubborn resolution of treating the whole thing as an empty, meaningless dream, the effect of my overstrained mind, took possession of me. Yes; it was but a lying vision, an idiotic cheating of my own senses, suggesting pictures of death and misery which had been evoked by weeks of incertitude and mental depression.

"How could I see all that I have seen in less than half a minute?"—I exclaimed. "The theory of dreams, the rapidity with which the material changes on which our ideas in vision depend, are excited in the hemispherical ganglia, is sufficient to account for the long series of events I have seemed to experience. In dream alone can the relations of space and time be so completely annihilated. The *Yamabooshi* is for nothing in this disagreeable nightmare. He is only reaping that which has been sown by myself, and, by using some infernal drug, of which his tribe have the secret, he has contrived to make me lose consciousness for a few seconds and see that vision—as lying as it is horrid. *Avaunt* all such thoughts, I believe them not. In a few days there will be a steamer sailing for Europe. . . . I shall leave tomorrow!"

This disjointed monologue was pronounced by me aloud, regardless of the presence of my respected friend the Bonze, Tamoora, and the *Yamabooshi*. The latter was standing before me in the same position as when he placed the mirror in my hands, and kept looking at me calmly, I should perhaps say looking *through* me, and in dignified silence. The Bonze, whose kind countenance was beaming with sympathy, approached me as he would a sick child, and gently laying his hand on mine, and with tears in his eyes, said: "Friend, you must not leave this city before you have been completely purified of your contact with the lower *Daij-Dzins* (spirits), who had to be used to guide your inexperienced soul to the places it craved to see. The entrance to your Inner Self must be closed against their dangerous intrusion. Lose no time, therefore, my son, and allow the holy Master yonder, to purify you at once."

But nothing can be more deaf than anger once aroused. "The sap of reason" could no longer "quench the fire of passion," and at that moment I was not fit to listen to his friendly voice. His is a face I can never recall to my memory without genuine feeling; his, a name I will ever pronounce with a sigh of emotion; but at that ever memorable hour when my passions were inflamed to white heat, I felt almost a hatred for the kind, good old man, I could not forgive him his interference in the present event. Hence, for all answer, therefore, he received from me a stern rebuke, a violent protest on my part against the idea that I could ever regard the vision I had had, in any other light save that of an empty dream, and his *Yamabooshi* as anything better than an impostor. "I will leave tomorrow, had I to forfeit my whole fortune as a penalty"—I exclaimed, pale with rage and despair.

"You will repent it the whole of your life, if you do so before the holy man has shut every entrance in you against intruders ever on the watch and ready to enter the open door," was the answer. "The *Daij-Dzins* will have the best of you."

I interrupted him with a brutal laugh, and a still more brutally phrased inquiry about the *fees* I was expected to give the *Yamabooshi*, for his experiment with me.

"He needs no reward," was the reply. "The order he belongs to is the richest in the world, since its adherents need nothing, for they are above all terrestrial and venal desires. Insult him not, the good man who came to help you out of pure sympathy for your suffering, and to relieve you of mental agony."

But I would listen to no words of reason and wisdom. The spirit of rebellion and pride had taken possession of me, and made me disregard every feeling of personal friendship, or even of simple propriety. Luckily for me, on turning round to order the mendicant monk out of my presence, I found he had gone.

I had not seen him move, and attributed his stealthy departure to fear at having been detected and understood.

Fool! blind, conceited idiot that I was! Why did I fail to recognise the *Yamabooshi's* power, and that the peace of my whole life was departing with him, from that moment for ever? But I did so fail. Even the fell demon of my long fears—uncertainty—was now entirely overpowered by that fiend scepticism—the silliest of all. A dull, morbid unbelief, a stubborn denial of the evidence of my own senses, and a determined will to regard the whole vision as a fancy of my overwrought mind, had taken firm hold of me.

"My mind," I argued, "what is it? Shall I believe with the superstitious and the weak that this production of phosphorus and gray matter is indeed the superior part of me; that it can act and see independently of my physical senses? Never! As well believe in the planetary 'intelligences' of the astrologer, as in the 'Daij-Dzins' of my credulous though well-meaning friend, the priest. As well confess one's belief in Jupiter and Sol, Saturn and Mercury, and that these worthies guide their spheres and concern themselves with mortals, as to give one serious thought to the airy nonentities supposed to have guided my 'soul' in its unpleasant dream! I loathe and laugh at the absurd idea. I regard it as a personal insult to the intellect and rational reasoning powers of a man, to speak of invisible creatures, '*subjective* intelligences,' and all that kind of insane superstition." In short, I begged my friend the Bonze to spare me his protests, and thus the unpleasantness of breaking with him for ever.

Thus I raved and argued before the venerable Japanese gentleman, doing all in my power to leave on his mind the indelible conviction of my having gone suddenly mad. But his admirable forbearance proved more than equal to my idiotic passion; and he implored me once more, for the sake of my whole future, to submit to certain "necessary purificatory rites."

"Never! Far rather dwell in air, rarefied to nothing by the air-pump of wholesome unbelief, than in the dim fog of silly superstition," I argued, paraphrasing Richter's remark. "I will not believe," I repeated; "but as I can no longer bear such uncertainty about my sister and her family, I will return by the first steamer to Europe."

This final determination upset my old acquaintance altogether. His earnest prayer not to depart before I had seen the *Yamabooshi* once more, received no attention from me.

"Friend of a foreign land!"—he cried, "I pray that you may not repent of your unbelief and rashness. May the 'Holy One' (Kwan-On, the Goddess of Mercy) protect you from the *Dzins*! For, since you refuse to submit to the process of purification at the hands of the holy *Yamabooshi*, he is powerless to defend you from the evil influences evoked by your unbelief and defiance of truth. But let me, at this parting hour, I beseech you, let me, an older man who wishes you well, warn you once more and persuade you of things you are still ignorant of. May I speak?"

"Go on and have your say," was the ungracious assent. "But let me warn you, in my turn, that nothing you can say can make of me a believer in your disgraceful superstitions." This was added with a cruel feeling of pleasure in bestowing one more needless insult.

But the excellent man disregarded this new sneer as he had all others. Never shall I forget the solemn earnestness of his parting words, the pitying, remorseful look on his face when he found that it was, indeed, all to no purpose, that by his kindly meant interference he had only led me to my destruction.

"Lend me your ear, good sir, for the last time," he began,

"learn that unless the holy and venerable man, who, to relieve your distress, opened your 'soul vision,' is permitted to complete his work, your future life will, indeed, be little worth living. He has to safeguard you against involuntary repetitions of visions of the same character. Unless you consent to it of your own free will, however, you will have to be left in the power of *Forces* which will harass and persecute you to the verge of insanity. Know that the development of 'Long Vision' (clairvoyance)—which is accomplished *at will* only by those for whom the Mother of Mercy, the great Kwan-On, has no secrets—must, in the case of the beginner, be pursued with help of the air *Dzins* (elemental spirits) whose nature is soulless, and hence wicked.

"Know also that, while the *Arihat*, 'the destroyer of the enemy,' who has subjected and made of these creatures his servants, has nothing to fear; he who has no power over them becomes their slave. Nay, laugh not in your great pride and ignorance, but listen further. During the time of the vision and while the inner perceptions are directed towards the events they seek, the *Daij-Dzin* has the seer—when, like yourself, he is an inexperienced tyro—entirely in its power; and for the time being *that seer is no longer himself.* He partakes of the nature of his 'guide.'

"The *Daij-Dzin*, which directs his inner sight, keeps his soul in durance vile, making of him, while the state lasts, a creature like itself. Bereft of his divine light, man is but a soulless being; hence during the time of such connection, he will feel no human emotions, neither pity nor fear, love nor mercy."

"Hold!" I involuntarily exclaimed, as the words vividly brought back to my recollection the indifference with which I had witnessed my sister's despair and sudden loss of reason in my "hallucination."

"Hold! . . . But no; it is still worse madness in me to heed or find any sense in your ridiculous tale! But if you knew it to be so dangerous why have advised the experiment at all?"—I added mockingly.

"It had to last but a few seconds, and no evil could have resulted from it, had you kept your promise to submit to purification," was the sad and humble reply. "I wished you well, my friend, and my heart was nigh breaking to see you suffering day by day. The experiment is harmless when directed by *one who knows*, and becomes dangerous only when the final precaution is neglected. It is the 'Master of Visions,' he who has opened an entrance into your soul, who has to close it by using the Seal of Purification against any further and deliberate ingress of. . . ."

"The 'Master of Visions,' forsooth!" I cried, brutally interrupting him, "say rather the Master of Imposture!"

The look of sorrow on his kind old face was so intense and painful to behold that I perceived I had gone too far; but it was too late.

"Farewell, then!" said the old bonze, rising; and after performing the usual ceremonials of politeness, Tamoora left the house in dignified silence.

6: I Depart—But Not Alone

Several days later I sailed, but during my stay I saw my venerable friend the Bonze, no more. Evidently on that last, and to me for ever memorable evening, he had been seriously offended with my more than irreverent, my downright insulting remark about one whom he so justly respected. I felt sorry for him, but the wheel of passion and pride was too incessantly at work to permit me to feel a single moment of remorse. What was it that made me so relish the pleasure of wrath, that when, for one instant, I happened to lose sight of my supposed grievance toward the *Yamabooshi*, I forthwith lashed myself back into a kind of artificial fury against him. He had only accomplished what he had been expected to do, and what he had tacitly promised; not only so, but it was I myself who had deprived him of the possibility of doing more, even for my own protection, if I might believe the Bonze—a man whom I knew to be thoroughly honourable and reliable. Was it regret at having been forced by my pride to refuse the proffered precaution, or was it the fear of remorse that made me rake together, in my heart, during those evil hours, the smallest details of the supposed insult to that same suicidal pride? Remorse, as an old poet has aptly remarked:

". . .is like the heart in which it grows: . . .
. . . if proud and gloomy,
It is a poison-tree, that pierced to the utmost,
Weeps only tears of blood."

Perchance, it was the indefinite fear of something of that sort which caused me to remain so obdurate, and led me to excuse, under the plea of terrible provocation, even the unprovoked insults that I had heaped upon the head of my kind and all-forgiving friend, the priest. However, it was now too late in the day to recall the words of offence I had uttered; and all I could do was to promise myself the satisfaction of writing him a friendly letter, as soon as I reached home. Fool, blind fool, elated with insolent self-conceit, that I was! So sure did I feel, that my vision was due merely to some trick of the *Yamabooshi*, that I actually gloated over my coming triumph in writing to the Bonze that I had been right in answering his sad words of parting with an incredulous smile, as my sister and family were all in good health—happy!

I had not been at sea for a week, before I had cause to remember his words of warning!

From the day of my experience with the magic mirror, I perceived a great change in my whole state, and I attributed it, at first, to the mental depression I had struggled against for so many months. During the day I very often found myself absent from the surrounding scenes, losing sight for several minutes of things and persons. My nights were disturbed, my dreams oppressive, and at times horrible. Good sailor I certainly was; and besides, the weather was unusually fine, the ocean as smooth as a pond. Notwithstanding this, I often felt a strange giddiness, and the familiar faces of my fellow-passengers assumed at such times the most grotesque appearances.

Thus, a young German I used to know well was once suddenly transformed before my eyes into his old father, whom we had laid in the little burial place of the European colony some three years before. We were talking on deck of the defunct and of a certain business arrangement of his, when Max Grunner's head appeared to me as though it were covered with a strange film. A thick greyish mist surrounded him, and gradually condensing around and upon his healthy countenance, settled suddenly into the grim old head I had myself seen covered with six feet of soil.

On another occasion, as the captain was talking of a Malay thief whom he had helped to secure and lodge in jail, I saw near him the yellow, villainous face of a man answering to his description. I kept silence about such hallucinations; but as they became more and more frequent, I felt very much disturbed, though still attributing them to natural causes, such as I had read about in medical books.

One night I was abruptly wakened by a long and loud cry of distress. It was a woman's voice, plaintive like that of a child, full of terror and of helpless despair. I awoke with a start to find myself on land, in a strange room. A young girl, almost a child, was desperately struggling against a powerful middle-aged man, who had surprised her in her own room, and during her sleep. Behind the closed and locked door, I saw listening an old woman, whose face, notwithstanding the fiendish expression upon it, seemed familiar to me, and I immediately recognised it: it was the face of the Jewess who had adopted my niece in the dream I had at Kioto. She had received gold to pay for her share in the foul crime, and was now keeping her part of the covenant.... But who was the victim? O horror unutterable! Unspeakable horror! When I realised the situation after coming back to my normal state, I found it was my own child-niece.

But, as in my first vision, I felt in me nothing of the nature of that despair born of affection that fills one's heart, at the sight of a wrong done to, or a misfortune befalling, those one loves; nothing but a manly indignation in the presence of suffering inflicted upon the weak and the helpless. I rushed, of course, to her rescue, and seized the wanton, brutal beast by the neck. I fastened upon him with powerful grasp, but, the man heeded it not, he seemed not even to feel my hand.

The coward, seeing himself resisted by the girl, lifted his powerful arm, and the thick fist, coming down like a heavy hammer upon the sunny locks, felled the child to the ground. It was with a loud cry of the indignation of a stranger, not with that of a tigress defending her cub, that I sprang upon the lewd beast and sought to throttle him. I then remarked, for the first time, that, a shadow myself, I was grasping but another shadow! . . . .

My loud shrieks and imprecations had awakened the whole steamer. They were attributed to a nightmare. I did not seek to take anyone into my confidence; but, from that day forward, my life became a long series of mental tortures, I could hardly shut my eyes without becoming witness of some horrible deed, some scene of misery, death or crime, whether past, present or even future—as I ascertained later on. It was as though some mocking fiend had taken upon himself the task of making me go through the vision of everything that was bestial, malignant and hopeless, in this world of misery.

No radiant vision of beauty or virtue ever lit with the faintest ray these pictures of awe and wretchedness that I seemed doomed to witness. Scenes of wickedness, of murder, of treachery and of lust fell dismally upon my sight, and I was brought face to face with the vilest results of man's passions, the most terrible outcome of his material earthly cravings.

Had the Bonze foreseen, indeed, the dreary results, when he spoke of *Daij-Dzins* to whom I left "an ingress" "a door open" in me? Nonsense! There must be some physiological, abnormal change in me. Once at Nuremberg, when I have ascertained how false was the direction taken by my fears—I dared not hope for no misfortune at all—these meaningless visions will disappear as they came. The very fact that my fancy follows but one direction, that of pictures of misery, of human passions in their worst, material shape, is a proof to me, of their unreality.

"If, as you say, man consists of one substance, matter, the object of the physical senses; and if perception with its modes is only the result of the organization of the brain, then should

41

we be naturally attracted but to the material, the earthly".... I thought I heard the familiar voice of the Bonze interrupting my reflections, and repeating an often used argument of his in his discussions with me.

"There are two planes of visions before men," I again heard him say, "the plane of undying love and spiritual aspirations, the efflux from the eternal light; and the plane of restless, ever changing matter, the light in which the misguided *Daij-Dzins* bathe."

7: ETERNITY IN A SHORT DREAM

In those days I could hardly bring myself to realise, even for a moment, the absurdity of a belief in any kind of spirits, whether good or bad. I now understood, if I did not believe, what was meant by the term, though I still persisted in hoping that it would finally prove some physical derangement or nervous hallucination. To fortify my unbelief the more, I tried to bring back to my memory all the arguments used against a faith in such superstitions, that I had ever read or heard. I recalled the biting sarcasms of Voltaire, the calm reasoning of Hume, and I repeated to myself *ad nauseam* the words of Rousseau, who said that superstition, "the disturber of Society," could never be too strongly attacked. "Why should the sight, the phantasmagoria, rather"—I argued—"of that which we know in a waking sense to be false, come to affect us at all?" Why should—

Names, whose sense we see not
Fray us with things that be not?

One day the old captain was narrating to us the various superstitions to which sailors were addicted; a pompous English missionary remarked that Fielding had declared long ago that "superstition renders a man a fool,"—after which he hesitated for an instant, and abruptly stopped. I had not taken any part in the general conversation; but no sooner had the reverend speaker relieved himself of the quotation, than I saw in that halo of vibrating light, which I now noticed almost constantly over every human head on the steamer, the words of Fielding's next proposition—"and *scepticism makes him mad.*"

I had heard and read of the claims of those who pretend to seership, that they often see the thoughts of people traced in the aura of those present. Whatever "aura" may mean with others, I had now a personal experience of the truth of the claim, and felt sufficiently disgusted with the discovery! I—a *clairvoyant!* a new horror added to my life, an absurd and ridiculous gift developed, which I shall have to conceal from all, feeling ashamed of it as if it were a case of leprosy. At this moment my hatred to the *Yama-booshi*, and even to my venerable old friend, the Bonze, knew no bounds. The former had evidently by his manipulations over me while I was lying unconscious, touched some unknown physiological spring in my brain, and by loosing it had called forth a faculty generally hidden in the human constitution; and it was the Japanese priest who had introduced the wretch into my house!

But my anger and my curses were alike useless, and could be of no avail. Moreover, we were already in European waters, and in a few more days we should be at Hamburg. Then would my doubts and fears be set at rest, and I should find, to my intense relief, that although clairvoyance, as regards the reading of human thoughts on the spot, may have some truth in it, the discernment of such events at a distance, as I had *dreamed of*, was an impossibility for human faculties. Notwithstanding all my reasoning, however, my heart was sick with fear, and full of the blackest presentiments; I *felt* that my doom was closing. I suffered terribly, my nervous and mental prostration becoming intensified day by day.

The night before we entered port I had a dream.

I fancied I was dead. My body lay cold and stiff in its last sleep, whilst its dying consciousness, which still regarded itself as "I," realising the event, was preparing to meet in a few seconds its own extinction. It had been always my belief that as the brain preserved heat longer than any of the other organs, and was the last to cease its activity, the thought in it survived bodily death by several minutes. Therefore, I was not in the least surprised to find in my dream that while the frame had already crossed that awful gulf "*no mortal e'er repassed*," its consciousness was still in the gray twilight, the first shadows of the great Mystery. Thus my *thought* wrapped, as I believed, in the remnants, of its now fast retiring vitality, was watching with intense and eager curiosity the approaches of its own dissolution, *i.e.*, of its *annihilation*.

"I" was hastening to record my last impressions, lest the dark mantle of eternal oblivion should envelope me, before I had time to feel and *enjoy*, the great, the supreme triumph of learning that my life-long convictions were true, that death is a complete and absolute cessation of conscious being. Everything around me was getting darker with every moment. Huge gray shadows were moving before my vision, slowly at first, then with accelerated motion, until they commenced whirling around with an almost vertiginous rapidity.

Then, as though that motion had taken place only for purposes of brewing darkness, the object once reached, it slackened its speed, and as the darkness became gradually transformed into intense blackness, it ceased altogether. There was nothing now within my immediate perceptions, but that fathomless black Space, as dark as pitch: to me it appeared as limitless and as silent as the shoreless Ocean of Eternity upon which Time, the progeny of man's brain, is for ever gliding, but which it can never cross.

Dream is defined by Cato as "but the image of our hopes and fears." Having never feared death when awake, I felt, in this dream of mine, calm and serene at the idea of my speedy end. In truth, I felt rather relieved at the thought—probably owing to my recent mental suffering—that the end of all, of doubt, of fear for those I loved, of suffering, and of every anxiety, was close at hand. The constant anguish that had been gnawing ceaselessly at my heavy, aching heart for many a long and weary month, had now become unbearable; and if as Seneca thinks, death is but "*the ceasing to be what we were before*," it was better that I should die.

The body is dead; "I," its consciousness—that which is all that remains of me now, for a few moments longer—am preparing to follow. Mental perceptions will get weaker, more dim and hazy with every second of time, until the longed for oblivion envelopes me completely in its cold shroud. Sweet is the magic hand of Death, the great World-Comforter; profound and dreamless is sleep in its unyielding arms. Yea, verily, it is a welcome guest.... A calm and peaceful haven amidst the roaring billows of the Ocean of life, whose breakers lash in vain the rock-bound shores of Death. Happy the lonely bark that drifts into the still waters of its black gulf, after having been so long, so cruelly tossed about by the angry waves of sentient life. Moored in it for evermore, needing no longer either sail or rudder, my bark will now find rest. Welcome then, O Death, at this tempting price; and fare thee well, poor body, which, having neither sought it nor derived pleasure from it, I now readily give up! ...

While uttering this death-chant to the prostrate form before me, I bent over, and examined it with curiosity. I felt the surrounding darkness oppressing me, weighing on me almost tangibly, and I fancied I found in it the approach of the Liberator I was welcoming. And yet .. how very strange! If real, final Death takes place in our consciousness; if after the bodily death, "I" and my conscious perceptions are one—how is it that these perceptions do not become weaker, why does my *brain*-action seem as vigorous as ever now ... that I am *de facto* dead? ...

Nor does the usual feeling of anxiety, the "heavy heart" so-called, decrease in intensity; nay, it even seems to become worse ... unspeakably so! ... How long it takes for full oblivion to arrive! ...Ah, here's my body again!...Vanished out of sight for a second or two, it reappears before me once more.... How white and ghastly it looks! Yet ... its brain cannot be quite dead, since "I," its consciousness, am still acting, since we two fancy that we still are, that we live and think, disconnected from our creator and its ideating cell.

Suddenly I felt a strong desire to see how much longer the progress of dissolution was likely to last, before it placed its last seal on the brain and rendered it inactive. I examined my brain in its cranial cavity, through the (to me) entirely transparent walls and roof of the skull, and even *touched the brain-matter*. . . . How, or with *whose hands*, I am now unable to say; but the impression of the slimy, intensely cold matter produced a very strong impression on me, in that dream.

To my great dismay, I found that the blood having entirely congealed and the brain-tissues having themselves undergone a change that would no longer permit any molecular action, it became impossible for me to account for the phenomena now taking place with myself. Here was I,—or my consciousness, which is all one—standing apparently entirely disconnected from my brain which could no longer function. . . . But I had no time left for reflection. A new and most extraordinary change in my perceptions had taken place and now engrossed my whole attention. . . . What *does* this signify? . . .

The same darkness was around me as before, a black, impenetrable space, extending in every direction. Only now, right before me, in whatever direction I was looking, moving with me which way soever I moved, there was a gigantic round clock; a disk, whose large white face shone ominously on the ebony-black background. As I looked at its huge dial, and at the pendulum moving to and fro regularly and slowly in Space, as if its swinging meant to divide eternity, I saw its needles pointing to *seven minutes past five*. "The hour at which my torture had commenced at Kioto!" I had barely found time to think of the coincidence, when, to my unutterable horror, I felt myself going through the same, the identical, process that I had been made to experience on that memorable and fatal day.

I swam underground, dashing swiftly through the earth; I found myself once more in the pauper's grave and recognised my brother-in-law in the mangled remains; I witnessed his terrible death; entered my sister's house; followed her agony, and saw her go mad. I went over the same scenes without missing a single detail of them. But, alas! I was no longer iron-bound in the calm indifference that had then been mine, and which in that first vision had left me as unfeeling to my great misfortune as if I had been a heartless thing of rock. My mental tortures were now becoming beyond description and well-nigh unbearable.

Even the settled despair, the never ceasing anxiety I was constantly experiencing when awake, had become now, in my dream and in the face of this repetition of visions and events, as an hour of darkened sunlight compared to a deadly cyclone. Oh! how I suffered in this wealth and pomp of infernal horrors, to which the conviction of the survival of man's consciousness after death—for in that dream I firmly believed that my body was dead—added the most terrifying of all!

The relative relief I felt, when, after going over the last scene, I saw once more the great white face of the dial before me was not of long duration. The long, arrow-shaped needle was pointing on the colossal disk at—*seven minutes and a-half past five* o'clock. But, before I had time to well realise the change, the needle moved slowly backwards, stopped at precisely the seventh minute, and—O cursed fate!. . . I found myself driven into a repetition of the same series over again! Once more I swam underground, and saw, and heard, and suffered every torture that hell can provide; I passed through every mental anguish known to man or fiend.

I returned to see the fatal dial and its needle—after what appeared to me an eternity—moved, as before, only half a minute forward. I beheld it, with renewed terror, moving back again, and felt myself propelled forward anew. And so it went on, and on, and on, time after time, in what seemed to me an endless succession, a series which never had any beginning, nor would it ever have an end. . . .

Worst of all; my consciousness, my "I," had apparently acquired the phenomenal capacity of trebling, quadrupling, and even of decuplating itself. I lived, felt and suffered, in the same space of time, in half-a-dozen different places at once, passing over various events of my life, at different epochs, and under the most dissimilar circumstances; though predominant over all was my *spiritual* experience at Kioto. Thus, as in the famous *fugue* in

Don Giovanni, the heart-rending notes of Elvira's *aria* of despair ring high above, but interfere in no way with the melody of the minuet, the song of seduction, and the chorus, so I went over and over my travailed woes, the feelings of agony unspeakable at the awful sights of my vision, the repetition of which blunted in no wise even a single pang of my despair and horror; nor did these feelings weaken in the least scenes and events entirely disconnected with the first one, that I was living through again, or interfere in any way the one with the other. It was a maddening experience! A series of contrapuntal, mental phantasmagoria from real life.

Here was I, during the same half-a-minute of time, examining with cold curiosity the mangled remains of my sister's husband; following with the same indifference the effects of the news on her brain, as in my first Kioto vision, and feeling *at the same time* hell-torture for these very events, as when I returned to consciousness. I was listening to the philosophical discourses of the Bonze, every word of which I heard and understood, and was trying to laugh him to scorn. I was again a child, then a youth, hearing my mother's and my sweet sister's voices, admonishing me and teaching duty to all men. I was saving a friend from drowning, and was sneering at his aged father who thanks me for having saved a "soul" yet unprepared to meet his Maker.

"Speak of *dual* consciousness, you psycho-physiologists!"— I cried, in one of the moments when agony, mental and as it seemed to me physical also, had arrived at a degree of intensity which would have killed a dozen living men; "speak of your psychological and physiological experiments, you schoolmen, puffed up with pride and book-learning! Here am I to give you the lie. . . ." And now I was reading the works and holding converse with learned professors and lecturers, who had led me to my fatal scepticism. And, while arguing the impossibility of consciousness divorced from its brain, I was shedding tears of blood over the supposed fate of my nieces and nephews.

More terrible than all: I knew, *as only a liberated consciousness can know*, that all I had seen in my vision at Japan, and all that

I was seeing and hearing over and over again now, was true in every point and detail, that it was a long string of ghastly and terrible, still of real, actual, facts.

For, perhaps, the hundredth time, I had riveted my attention on the needle of the clock, I had lost the number of my gyrations and was fast coming to the conclusion that they would never stop, that consciousness, is, after all, indestructible, and that this was to be my punishment in Eternity. I was beginning to realise from personal experience how the condemned sinners would feel—"were not eternal damnation a logical and mathematical impossibility in an ever progressing Universe"—I still found the force to argue. Yea, indeed; at this hour of my ever-increasing agony, my consciousness—now my synonym for "I"—had still the power of revolting at certain theological claims, of denying all their propositions, all—save *itself*. . . . No; I denied the independent nature of my consciousness no longer, for I knew it now to be such.

But is it *eternal* withal? O thou incomprehensible and terrible Reality! But if thou art eternal, who then art thou?—since there is no deity, no God. Whence dost thou come, and when didst thou first appear, if thou art not a part of the cold body lying yonder? And whither dost thou lead me, who am thyself, and shall our thought and fancy have an end? What is thy real name, thou unfathomable *reality*, and impenetrable *mystery!* Oh, I would fain annihilate thee. . . . "Soul-Vision"!—who speaks of Soul, and whose voice is this? . . . It says that I see now for myself, that there is a Soul in man, after all. . . . I deny this. My Soul, my vital Soul, or the Spirit of life, has expired with my body, with the gray matter of my brain. This "I" of mine, this consciousness, is not yet proven to me as eternal. Reincarnation, in which the Bonze felt so anxious I should believe may be true. . . . Why not? Is not the flower born year after year from the same root? Hence this "I" once separated from its brain, losing its balance, and calling forth such a host of visions. . . . before reincarnating. . . .

I was again face to face with the inexorable, fatal clock. And as I was watching its needle, I heard the voice of the Bonze, coming out of the depths of its white face, saying: "In this case, I fear, *you would only have to open and to shut the temple door, over and over again, during a period which, however short, would seem to you an eternity.*" . . . .

The clock had vanished, darkness made room for light, the voice of my old friend was drowned by a multitude of voices overhead on deck; and I awoke in my berth, covered with a cold perspiration, and faint with terror.

8: TALE OF WOE

We were at Hamburg, and no sooner had I seen my partners, who could hardly recognise me, than with their consent and good wishes I started for Nuremberg.

Half-an-hour after my arrival, the last doubt with regard to the correctness of my vision had disappeared. The reality was worse than any expectations could have made it, and I was henceforward doomed to the most desolate life. I ascertained that I had seen the terrible tragedy with all its heartrending details. My brother-in-law, killed under the wheels of a machine; my sister, insane, and now rapidly sinking towards her end; my niece—the sweet flower of nature's fairest work—dishonoured, in a den of infamy; the little children dead of a contagious disease in an orphanage; my last surviving nephew at sea, no one knew where. A whole house, a home of love and peace, scattered; and I, left alone, a witness of this world of death, of desolation and dishonour.

The news filled me with infinite despair, and I sank helpless before this wholesale, dire disaster, which rose before me all at once. The shock proved too much, and I fainted. The last thing I heard before entirely losing my consciousness was a remark of the *burgmeister*: "Had you, before leaving Kioto, telegraphed to the city authorities of your whereabouts, and of your intention of coming home to take charge of your young relatives, we might have placed them elsewhere, and thus have saved them from their fate. No one knew that the children had a well-to-do relative. They were left paupers and had to be dealt with as such.

They were comparatively strangers in Nuremberg, and under the unfortunate circumstances you could hardly have expected anything else. . . . I can only express my sincere sorrow."

It was this terrible knowledge that I might, at any rate, have saved my young niece from her unmerited fate, but that through my neglect I had not done so, that was killing me. Had I but followed the friendly advice of the Bonze, Tamoora, and telegraphed to the authorities some weeks previous to my return much might have been avoided. It was all this, coupled with the fact that I could no longer doubt clairvoyance and clairaudience—the possibility of which I had so long denied—that brought me so heavily down upon my knees. I could avoid the censure of my fellow-creatures, but I could never escape the stings of my conscience, the reproaches of my own aching heart—no, not as long as I lived. I cursed my stubborn scepticism, my denial of facts, my early education, I cursed myself, and the whole world. . . .

For several days I contrived not to sink beneath my load, for I had a duty to perform to the dead and to the living. But my sister once rescued from the pauper's asylum, placed under the care of the best physicians, with her daughter to attend to her last moments, and the Jewess, whom I had brought to confess her crime, safely lodged in jail—my fortitude and strength suddenly abandoned me. Hardly a week after my arrival I was myself no better than a raving maniac, helpless in the strong grip of a brain fever. For several weeks I lay between life and death, the terrible disease defying the skill of the best physicians. At last my strong constitution prevailed, and—to my life-long sorrow—they proclaimed me saved.

I heard the news with a bleeding heart. Doomed to drag the loathsome burden of life henceforth alone, and in constant remorse; hoping for no help or remedy on earth, and still refusing to believe in the possibility of anything better than a short survival of consciousness beyond the grave, this unexpected return to life added only one more drop of gall to my bitter feelings. They were hardly soothed by the immediate return, during the first days of my convalescence, of those unwelcome and un-sought for visions, whose correctness and reality I could deny no more. Alas the day! they were no longer in my sceptical, blind mind—

The children of an idle brain
Begot of nothing but vain fantasy;

. . . but always the faithful photographs of the real woes and sufferings of my fellow creatures, of my best friends. . . . Thus I found myself doomed, whenever I was left for a moment alone, to the helpless torture of a chained Prometheus. During the still hours of night, as though held by some pitiless iron hand, I found myself led to my sister's bedside, forced to watch there hour after hour, and see the silent disintegration of her wasted organism; to witness and feel the sufferings that her own ten-antless brain could no longer reflect or convey to her percep-tions. But there was something still more horrible to barb the dart that could never be extricated. I had to look, by day, at the childish innocent face of my young niece, so sublimely simple and guileless in her pollution; and to witness, by night, how the full knowledge and recollection of her dishonour, of her young life now for ever blasted, came to her in her dreams, as soon as she was asleep.

These dreams took an objective form to me, as they had done on the steamer; I had to live them over again, night after night, and feel the same terrible despair. For now, since I believed in the reality of seership, and had come to the conclusion that in our bodies lies hidden, as in the caterpillar, the chrysalis which may contain in its turn the butterfly—the symbol of the soul—I no longer remained indifferent, as of yore, to what I witnessed in my Soul-life. Something had suddenly developed in me, had broken loose from its icy cocoon. Evidently I no longer saw only in consequence of the identification of my inner nature with a *Daij-Dzin*; my visions arose in consequence of a direct personal psychic development, the fiendish creatures only tak-ing care that I should see nothing of an agreeable or elevating nature.

Thus, now, not an unconscious pang in my dying sister's emaciated body, not a thrill of horror in my niece's restless sleep at the recollection of the crime perpetrated upon her, an innocent child, but found a responsive echo in my bleeding heart. The deep fountain of sympathetic love and sorrow had gushed out from the physical heart, and was now loudly echoed by the awakened soul separated from the body. Thus had I to drain the cup of misery to the very dregs! Woe is me, it was a daily and nightly torture! Oh, how I mourned over my proud folly; how I was punished for having neglected to avail myself at Kioto of the proffered purification, for now I had come to believe even in the efficacy of the latter. The *Daij-Dzin* had indeed obtained control over me; and the fiend had let loose all the dogs of hell upon his victim. . . .

At last the awful gulf was reached and crossed. The poor insane martyr dropped into her dark, and now welcome grave, leaving behind her, but for a few short months, her young, her first-born, daughter. Consumption made short work of that tender girlish frame. Hardly a year after my arrival, I was left alone in the whole wide world, my only surviving nephew having expressed a desire to follow his sea-faring career.

And now, the sequel of my sad, sad story is soon told. A wreck, a prematurely old man, looking at thirty as though sixty winters had passed over my doomed head, and owing to the never-ceasing visions, myself daily on the verge of insanity, I suddenly formed a desperate resolution. I would return to Kioto and seek out the *Yamabooshi*. I would prostrate myself at the feet of the holy man, and would not leave him until he had recalled the Frankenstein he had raised, the Frankenstein with whom at the time, it was I, myself, who would not part, through my insolent pride and unbelief.

Three months later I was in my Japanese home again, and I at once sought out my old, venerable Bonze, Tamoora Hideyeri, I now implored him to take me without an hour's delay, to the *Yamabooshi*, the innocent cause of my daily tortures. His answer

53

but placed the last, the supreme seal on my doom and tenfold intensified my despair. The *Yamabooshi* had left the country for lands unknown! He had departed one fine morning into the interior, on a pilgrimage, and according to custom, would be absent, unless natural death shortened the period, for no less than seven years! . . . .

In this mischance, I applied for help and protection to other learned *Yamabooshis*; and though well aware how useless it was in my case to seek efficient cure from any other "adept," my excellent old friend did everything he could to help me in my misfortune. But it was to no purpose, and the canker-worm of my life's despair could not be thoroughly extricated. I found from them that not one of these learned men could promise to relieve me entirely from the demon of clairvoyant obsession. It was he who raised certain *Daij-Dzins*, calling on them to show futurity, or things that had already come to pass, who alone had full control over them.

With kind sympathy, which I had now learned to appreciate, the holy men invited me to join the group of their disciples, and learn from them what I could do for myself. "Will alone, faith in your own soul powers, can help you now," they said. "But it may take several years to undo even a part of the great mischief;" they added. "A *Daij-Dzin* is easily dislodged in the beginning; if left alone, he takes possession of a man's nature, and it becomes almost impossible to uproot the fiend without killing his victim."

Persuaded that there was nothing but this left for me to do, I gratefully assented, doing my best to believe in all that these holy men believed in, and yet ever failing to do so in my heart. The demon of unbelief and all-denial seemed rooted in me more firmly even than the *Daij-Dzin*. Still I did all I could do, decided as I was not to lose my last chance of salvation. Therefore, I proceeded without delay to free myself from the world and my commercial obligations, in order to live for several years an independent life. I settled my accounts with my Hamburg partners and severed my connection with the firm. Notwithstanding considerable financial losses resulting from such a precipitate liquidation, I found myself, after closing the accounts, a far richer man than I had thought I was.

But wealth had no longer any attraction for me, now that I had no one to share it with, no one to work for. Life had become a burden; and such was my indifference to my future, that while giving away all my fortune to my nephew—in case he should return alive from his sea voyage—I should have neglected entirely even a small provision for myself, had not my native partner interfered and insisted upon my making it. I now recognised with Lao-tze, that Knowledge was the only firm hold for a man to trust to, as it is the only one that cannot be shaken by any tempest. Wealth is a weak anchor in days of sorrow, and self-conceit the most fatal counsellor.

Hence I followed the advice of my friends, and laid aside for myself a modest sum, which would be sufficient to assure me a small income for life, or if I ever left my new friends and instructors. Having settled my earthly accounts and disposed of my belongings at Kioto, I joined the "Masters of the Long Vision," who took me to their mysterious abode. There I remained for several years, studying very earnestly and in the most complete solitude, seeing no one but a few of the members of our religious community.

Many are the mysteries of nature that I have fathomed since then, and many a secret folio from the library of Tzion-ene have I devoured, obtaining thereby mastery over several kinds of invisible beings of a lower order. But the great secret of power over the terrible *Daij-Dzin* I could not get. It remains in the possession of a very limited number of the highest Initiates of Lao-tze, the great majority of the *Yamabooshis* themselves being ignorant how to obtain such mastery over the dangerous Elemental. One who would reach such power of control would have to become entirely identified with the *Yamabooshis*, to accept their views and beliefs, and to attain the highest degree of Initiation.

Very naturally, I was found unfit to join the Fraternity, owing to many insurmountable reasons besides my congenital and ineradicable scepticism, though I tried hard to believe. Thus, partially relieved of my affliction and taught how to conjure the unwelcome visions away, I still remained, and do remain to this day, helpless to prevent their forced appearance before me now and then.

It was after assuring myself of my unfitness for the exalted position of an independent Seer and Adept that I reluctantly gave up any further trial. Nothing had been heard of the holy man, the first innocent cause of my misfortune; and the old Bonze himself, who occasionally visited me in my retreat, either could not, or would not, inform me of the whereabouts of the *Yamabooshi*. When, therefore, I had to give up all hope of his ever relieving me entirely from my fatal gift, I resolved to return to Europe, to settle in solitude for the rest of my life. With this object in view, I purchased through my late partners the Swiss *châlet* in which my hapless sister and I were born, where I had grown up under her care, and selected it for my future hermitage.

When bidding me farewell for ever on the steamer which took me back to my fatherland, the good old Bonze tried to console me for my disappointments. "My son," he said, "regard all that happened to you as your *Karma*—a just retribution. No one who has subjected himself willingly to the power of a *Daij-Dzin* can ever hope to become a *Rahat* (an Adept), a high-souled *Yamabooshi*—unless immediately purified. At best, as in your case, he may become fitted to oppose and to successfully fight off the fiend. *Like a scar left after a poisonous wound, the trace of a Daij-Dzin can never be effaced from the Soul until purified by a new rebirth.* Withal, feel not dejected, but be of good cheer in your affliction, since it has led you to acquire true knowledge, and to accept many a truth you would have otherwise rejected with contempt.

And of this priceless knowledge, acquired through suffering and personal efforts—no *Daij-Dzin* can ever deprive you. Fare thee well, then, and may the Mother of Mercy, the great Queen of Heaven, afford you comfort and protection."

We parted, and since then I have led the life of an anchorite, in constant solitude and study. Though still occasionally afflicted, I do not regret the years I have passed under the instruction of the *Yamabooshis*, but feel gratified for the knowledge received. Of the priest Tamoora Hideyeri I think always with sincere affection and respect. I corresponded regularly with him to the day of his death; an event which, with all its to me painful details, I had the unthanked-for privilege of witnessing across the seas, at the very hour in which it occurred.

The Cave of the Echoes
A Strange But True Story

(This story is given from the narrative of an eye-witness, a Russian gentleman, very pious, and fully trustworthy. Moreover, the facts are copied from the police records of P——. The eyewitness in question attributes it, of course, partly to divine interference and partly to the Evil One.—H. P. B.)

In one of the distant governments of the Russian empire, in a small town on the borders of Siberia, a mysterious tragedy occurred more than thirty years ago. About six *versts* from the little town of P——, famous for the wild beauty of its scenery, and for the wealth of its inhabitants—generally proprietors of mines and of iron foundries—stood an aristocratic mansion. Its household consisted of the master, a rich old bachelor and his brother, who was a widower and the father of two sons and three daughters. It was known that the proprietor, Mr. Izvertzoff, had adopted his brother's children, and, having formed an especial attachment for his eldest nephew, Nicolas, he had made him the sole heir of his numerous estates.

Time rolled on. The uncle was getting old, the nephew was coming of age. Days and years had passed in monotonous serenity, when, on the hitherto clear horizon of the quiet family, appeared a cloud. On an unlucky day one of the nieces took it into her head to study the zither. The instrument being of purely Teutonic origin, and no teacher of it residing in the neighbourhood, the indulgent uncle sent to St. Petersburg for both. After diligent search only one professor could be found willing to trust himself in such close proximity to Siberia. It was an old German artist, who, sharing his affections equally between his instrument and a pretty blonde daughter, would part with neither. And thus it came to pass that one fine morning the old professor arrived at the mansion, with his music box under one arm and his fair Munchen leaning on the other.

From that day the little cloud began growing rapidly; for every vibration of the melodious instrument found a responsive echo in the old bachelor's heart. Music awakens love, they say, and the work begun by the zither was completed by Munchen's blue eyes. At the expiration of six months the niece had become an expert zither player, and the uncle was desperately in love.

One morning, gathering his adopted family around him, he embraced them all very tenderly, promised to remember them in his will, and wound up by declaring his unalterable resolution to marry the blue-eyed Munchen. After this he fell upon their necks and wept in silent rapture. The family, understanding that they were cheated out of the inheritance, also wept; but it was for another cause. Having thus wept, they consoled themselves and tried to rejoice, for the old gentleman was sincerely beloved by all. Not all of them rejoiced, though. Nicolas, who had himself been smitten to the heart by the pretty German, and who found himself defrauded at once of his *belle* and of his uncle's money, neither rejoiced nor consoled himself, but disappeared for a whole day.

Meanwhile, Mr. Izvertzoff had given orders to prepare his travelling carriage on the following day, and it was whispered that he was going to the chief town of the district, at some distance from his home, with the intention of altering his will. Though very wealthy, he had no superintendent on his estate, but kept his books himself. The same evening after supper, he was heard in his room, angrily scolding his servant, who had been in his service for over thirty years. This man, Ivan, was a native of northern Asia, from Kamschatka; he had been brought up by the family in the Christian religion, and was thought to be very much attached to his master.

A few days later, when the first tragic circumstance I am about to relate had brought all the police force to the spot, it was remembered that on that night Ivan was drunk; that his master, who had a horror of this vice had paternally thrashed him, and turned him out of his room, and that Ivan had been seen reeling out of the door, and had been heard to mutter threats.

On the vast domain of Mr. Izvertzoff there was a curious cavern, which excited the curiosity of all who visited it. It exists to this day, and is well known to every inhabitant of P——. A pine forest, commencing a few feet from the garden gate, climbs in steep terraces up a long range of rocky hills, which it covers with a broad belt of impenetrable vegetation. The grotto leading into the cavern, which is known as the "Cave of the Echoes," is situated about half a mile from the site of the mansion, from which it appears as a small excavation in the hill-side, almost hidden by luxuriant plants, but not so completely as to prevent any person entering it from being readily seen from the terrace in front of the house.

Entering the grotto, the explorer finds at the rear a narrow cleft; having passed through which he emerges into a lofty cavern, feebly lighted through fissures in the vaulted roof, fifty feet from the ground. The cavern itself is immense, and would easily hold between two and three thousand people. A part of it, in the days of Mr. Izvertzoff, was paved with flagstones, and was often used in the summer as a ball-room by picnic parties. Of an irregular oval, it gradually narrows into a broad corridor, which runs for several miles underground, opening here and there into other chambers, as large and lofty as the ball-room, but, unlike this, impassable otherwise than in a boat, as they are always full of water. These natural basins have the reputation of being unfathomable.

On the margin of the first of these is a small platform, with several mossy rustic seats arranged on it, and it is from this spot that the phenomenal echoes, which give the cavern its name, are heard in all their weirdness. A word pronounced in a whisper, or even a sigh, is caught up by endless mocking voices, and instead of diminishing in volume, as honest echoes do, the sound grows louder and louder at every successive repetition, until at last it bursts forth like the repercussion of a pistol shot, and recedes in a plaintive wail down the corridor.

On the day in question, Mr. Izvertzoff had mentioned his intention of having a dancing party in this cave on his wedding day, which he had fixed for an early date. On the following morning, while preparing for his drive, he was seen by his family entering the grotto, accompanied only by his Siberian servant. Half-an-hour later, Ivan returned to the mansion for a snuff-box, which his master had forgotten in his room, and went back with it to the cave. An hour later the whole house was startled by his loud cries. Pale and dripping with water, Ivan rushed in like a madman, and declared that Mr. Izvertzoff was nowhere to be found in the cave. Thinking he had fallen into the lake, he had dived into the first basin in search of him and was nearly drowned himself.

The day passed in vain attempts to find the body. The police filled the house, and louder than the rest in his despair was Nicolas, the nephew, who had returned home only to meet the sad tidings.

A dark suspicion fell upon Ivan, the Siberian. He had been struck by his master the night before, and had been heard to swear revenge. He had accompanied him alone to the cave, and when his room was searched, a box full of rich family jewellery, known to have been carefully kept in Mr. Izvertzoff's apartment, was found under Ivan's bedding. Vainly did the serf call God to witness that the box had been given to him in charge by his master himself, just before they proceeded to the cave; that it was the latter's purpose to have the jewellery reset, as he intended it for a wedding present to his bride; and that he, Ivan, would willingly give his own life to recall that of his master, if he knew him to be dead.

No heed was paid to him, however, and he was arrested and thrown into prison upon a charge of murder. There he was left, for under the Russian law a criminal cannot—at any rate, he could not in those days—be sentenced for a crime, however conclusive the circumstantial evidence, unless he confessed his guilt.

After a week had passed in useless search, the family arrayed themselves in deep mourning; and, as the will as originally drawn remained without a codicil, the whole of the property passed into the hands of the nephew. The old teacher and his daughter bore this sudden reverse of fortune with true Germanic phlegm, and prepared to depart. Taking again his zither under one arm, the old man was about to lead away his Munchen by the other, when the nephew stopped him by offering himself as the fair damsel's husband in the place of his departed uncle. The change was found to be an agreeable one, and, without much ado, the young people were married.

★★★★★★

Ten years rolled away, and we meet the happy family once more at the beginning of 1859. The fair Munchen had grown fat and vulgar. From the day of the old man's disappearance, Nicolas had become morose and retired in his habits, and many wondered at the change in him, for now he was never seen to smile. It seemed as if his only aim in life were to find out his uncle's murderer, or rather to bring Ivan to confess his guilt. But the man still persisted that he was innocent.

An only son had been born to the young couple, and a strange child it was. Small, delicate, and ever ailing, his frail life seemed to hang by a thread. When his features were in repose, his resemblance to his uncle was so striking that the members of the family often shrank from him in terror. It was the pale shrivelled face of a man of sixty upon the shoulders of a child nine years old. He was never seen either to laugh or to play, but, perched in his high chair, would gravely sit there, folding his arms in a way peculiar to the late Mr. Izvertzoff; and thus he would remain for hours, drowsy and motionless. His nurses were often seen furtively crossing themselves at night, upon approaching him, and not one of them would consent to sleep alone with him in the nursery.

His father's behaviour towards him was still more strange. He seemed to love him passionately, and at the same time to hate him bitterly. He seldom embraced or caressed the child, but, with livid cheek and staring eye, he would pass long hours watching him, as the child sat quietly in his corner, in his goblin-like, old-fashioned way.

The child had never left the estate, and few outside the family knew of his existence.

About the middle of July, a tall Hungarian traveller, preceded by a great reputation for eccentricity, wealth and mysterious powers, arrived at the town of P—— from the North, where, it was said, he had resided for many years. He settled in the little town, in company with a *Shaman* or South Siberian magician, on whom he was said to make mesmeric experiments. He gave dinners and parties, and invariably exhibited his *Shaman*, of whom he felt very proud, for the amusement of his guests. One day the notables of P—— made an unexpected invasion of the domains of Nicolas Izvertzoff, and requested the loan of his cave for an evening entertainment. Nicolas consented with great reluctance, and only after still greater hesitancy was he prevailed upon to join the party.

The first cavern and the platform beside the bottomless lake glittered with lights. Hundreds of flickering candles and torches, stuck in the clefts of the rocks, illuminated the place and drove the shadows from the mossy nooks and corners, where they had crouched undisturbed for many years. The stalactites on the walls sparkled brightly, and the sleeping echoes were suddenly awakened by a joyous confusion of laughter and conversation. The *Shaman*, who was never lost sight of by his friend and patron, sat in a corner, entranced as usual. Crouched on a projecting rock, about midway between the entrance and the water, with his lemon-yellow, wrinkled face, flat nose, and thin beard, he looked more like an ugly stone idol than a human being. Many of the company pressed around him and received correct answers to their questions, the Hungarian cheerfully submitting his mesmerized "subject" to cross-examination.

Suddenly one of the party, a lady, remarked that it was in that very cave that old Mr. Izvertzoff had so unaccountably disappeared ten years before. The foreigner appeared interested, and desired to learn more of the circumstances, so Nicolas was sought amid the crowd and led before the eager group. He was the host and he found it impossible to refuse the demanded narrative. He repeated the sad tale in a trembling voice, with a pallid cheek, and tears were seen glittering in his feverish eyes. The company were greatly affected, and encomiums upon the behaviour of the loving nephew in honouring the memory of his uncle and benefactor were freely circulating in whispers, when suddenly the voice of Nicolas became choked, his eyes started from their sockets, and with a suppressed groan, he staggered back. Every eye in the crowd followed with curiosity his haggard look, as it fell and remained riveted upon a weazened little face, that peeped from behind the back of the Hungarian.

"Where do you come from? Who brought you here, child?" gasped out Nicolas, as pale as death.

"I was in bed, papa; this man came to me, and brought me here in his arms," answered the boy simply, pointing to the *Shaman*, beside whom he stood upon the rock, and who, with his eyes closed, kept swaying himself to and fro like a living pendulum.

"That is very strange," remarked one of the guests, "for the man has never moved from his place."

"Good God! what an extraordinary resemblance!" muttered an old resident of the town, a friend of the lost man.

"You lie, child!" fiercely exclaimed the father. "Go to bed; this is no place for you."

"Come, come," interposed the Hungarian, with a strange expression on his face, and encircling with his arm the slender childish figure; "the little fellow has seen the double of my *Shaman*, which roams sometimes far away from his body, and has mistaken the phantom for the man himself. Let him remain with us for a while."

At these strange words the guests stared at each other in mute surprise, while some piously made the sign of the cross, spitting aside, presumably at the devil and all his works.

"By-the-bye," continued the Hungarian with a peculiar firmness of accent, and addressing the company rather than any one in particular; "why should we not try, with the help of my *Shaman*, to unravel the mystery hanging over the tragedy? Is the suspected party still lying in prison? What? he has not confessed up to now? This is surely very strange. But now we will learn the truth in a few minutes! Let all keep silent!"

He then approached the *Tehuktchene*, and immediately began his performance without so much as asking the consent of the master of the place. The latter stood rooted to the spot, as if petrified with horror, and unable to articulate a word. The suggestion met with general approbation, save from him; and the police inspector, Col. S——, especially approved of the idea.

"Ladies and gentlemen," said the mesmeriser in soft tones, "allow me for this once to proceed otherwise than in my general fashion. I will employ the method of native magic. It is more appropriate to this wild place, and far more effective as you will find, than our European method of mesmerisation."

Without waiting for an answer, he drew from a bag that never left his person, first a small drum, and then two little phials—one full of fluid, the other empty. With the contents of the former he sprinkled the *Shaman*, who fell to trembling and nodding more violently than ever. The air was filled with the perfume of spicy odours, and the atmosphere itself seemed to become clearer. Then, to the horror of those present, he approached the Tibetan, and taking a miniature stiletto from his pocket, he plunged the sharp steel into the man's forearm, and drew blood from it, which he caught in the empty phial.

When it was half filled, he pressed the orifice of the wound with his thumb, and stopped the flow of blood as easily as if he had corked a bottle, after which he sprinkled the blood over the little boy's head. He then suspended the drum from his neck, and, with two ivory drum-sticks, which were covered with magic signs and letters, he began beating a sort of *réveille*, to drum up the spirits, as he said.

The bystanders, half-shocked and half-terrified by these extraordinary proceedings, eagerly crowded round him, and for a few moments a dead silence reigned throughout the lofty cavern. Nicolas, with his face livid and corpse-like, stood speechless as before. The mesmeriser had placed himself between the *Shaman* and the platform, when he began slowly drumming. The first notes were muffled, and vibrated so softly in the air that they awakened no echo, but the *Shaman* quickened his pendulum-like motion and the child became restless. The drummer then began a slow chant, low, impressive and solemn.

As the unknown words issued from his lips, the flames of the candles and torches wavered and flickered, until they began dancing in rhythm with the chant. A cold wind came wheezing from the dark corridors beyond the water, leaving a plaintive echo in its trail. Then a sort of nebulous vapour, seeming to ooze from the rocky ground and walls, gathered about the Shaman and the boy. Around the latter the aura was silvery and transparent, but the cloud which enveloped the former was red and sinister.

Approaching nearer to the platform the magician beat a louder roll upon the drum, and this time the echo caught it up with terrific effect! It reverberated near and far in incessant peals; one wail followed another, louder and louder, until the thundering roar seemed the chorus of a thousand demon voices rising from the fathomless depths of the lake. The water itself, whose surface, illuminated by many lights, had previously been smooth as a sheet of glass, became suddenly agitated, as if a powerful gust of wind had swept over its unruffled face.

Another chant, and a roll of the drum, and the mountain trembled to its foundation with the cannon-like peals which rolled through the dark and distant corridors. The *Shaman's* body rose two yards in the air, and nodding and swaying, sat, self-suspended like an apparition. But the transformation which now occurred in the boy chilled everyone, as they speechlessly watched the scene. The silvery cloud about the boy now seemed to lift him, too, into the air; but, unlike the *Shaman*, his feet never left the ground. The child began to grow, as though the work of years was miraculously accomplished in a few seconds. He became tall and large, and his senile features grew older with the ageing of his body.

A few more seconds, and the youthful form had entirely disappeared. It was totally absorbed in another individuality, and to the horror of those present who had been familiar with his appearance, this individuality was that of old Mr. Izvertzoff, and on his temple was a large gaping wound, from which trickled great drops of blood.

This phantom moved towards Nicolas, till it stood directly in front of him, while he, with his hair standing erect, with the look of a madman gazed at his own son, transformed into his uncle. The sepulchral silence was broken by the Hungarian, who, addressing the child phantom, asked him in solemn voice:

"In the name of the great Master, of him who has all power, answer the truth, and nothing but the truth. Restless spirit, hast thou been lost by accident, or foully murdered?"

The spectre's lips moved, but it was the echo which answered for them in lugubrious shouts: "Murdered! murdered!! mur-der-ed!!!"

"Where? How? By whom?" asked the conjuror.

The apparition pointed a finger at Nicolas and, without removing its gaze or lowering its arm, retreated backwards slowly towards the lake. At every step it took, the younger Izvertzoff, as if compelled by some irresistible fascination, advanced a step towards it, until the phantom reached the lake, and the next moment was seen gliding on its surface. It was a fearful, ghostly scene!

When he had come within two steps of the brink of the watery abyss, a violent convulsion ran through the frame of the guilty man. Flinging himself upon his knees, he clung to one of the rustic seats with a desperate clutch, and staring wildly, uttered a long piercing cry of agony. The phantom now remained motionless on the water, and bending its extended finger, slowly

68

beckoned him to come. Crouched in abject terror, the wretched man shrieked until the cavern rang again and again: "I did not. . . . No, I did not murder you!"

Then came a splash, and now it was the boy who was in the dark water, struggling for his life, in the middle of the lake, with the same motionless stern apparition brooding over him.

"Papa! papa! Save me. . . . . I am drowning!" . . . . cried a piteous little voice amid the uproar of the mocking echoes.

"My boy!" shrieked Nicolas, in the accents of a maniac, springing to his feet. "My boy! Save him! Oh, save him! . . . . Yes, I confess. . . . I am the murderer. . . . It is I who killed him!"

Another splash, and the phantom disappeared. With a cry of horror the company rushed towards the platform; but their feet were suddenly rooted to the ground, as they saw amid the swirling eddies a whitish shapeless mass holding the murderer and the boy in tight embrace, and slowly sinking into the bottomless lake.

On the morning after these occurrences, when, after a sleepless night, some of the party visited the residence of the Hungarian gentleman, they found it closed and deserted. He and the *Shaman* had disappeared. Many are among the old inhabitants of P—— who remember him; the police inspector, Col. S——, dying a few years ago in the full assurance that the noble traveller was the devil. To add to the general consternation the Izvertzoff mansion took fire on that same night and was completely destroyed. The archbishop performed the ceremony of exorcism, but the locality is considered accursed to this day. The government investigated the facts, and—ordered silence.

The Luminous Shield
A.k.a. The Luninous Circle

We were a small and select party of light-hearted travellers. We had arrived at Constantinople a week before from Greece, and had devoted fourteen hours a day ever since to toiling up and down the steep heights of Pera, visiting bazaars, climbing to the tops of minarets and fighting our way through armies of hungry dogs, the traditional masters of the streets of Stamboul. Nomadic life is infectious, they say, and no civilization is strong enough to destroy the charm of unrestrained freedom when it has once been tasted. The gipsy cannot be tempted from his tent, and even the common tramp finds a fascination in his comfort-less and precarious existence, that prevents him taking to any fixed abode and occupation.

To guard my spaniel Ralph from falling a victim to this infec-tion, and joining the canine Bedouins that infested the streets, was my chief care during our stay in Constantinople. He was a fine fellow, my constant companion and cherished friend. Afraid of losing him, I kept a strict watch over his movements; for the first three days, however, he behaved like a tolerably well-educated quadruped, and remained faithfully at my heels. At every impudent attack from his Mahomedan cousins, whether intended as a hostile demonstration or an overture of friendship, his only reply would be to draw in his tail between his legs, and with an air of dignified modesty seek protection under the wing of one or other of our party.

As he had thus from the first shown so decided an aversion

to bad company, I began to feel assured of his discretion, and by the end of the third day I had considerably relaxed my vigilance. This carelessness on my part, however, was soon punished, and I was made to regret my misplaced confidence. In an unguarded moment he listened to the voice of some four-footed siren, and the last I saw of him was the end of his bushy tail, vanishing round the corner of a dirty, winding little back street.

Greatly annoyed, I passed the remainder of the day in a vain search after my dumb companion. I offered twenty, thirty, forty *francs* reward for him. About as many vagabond Maltese began a regular chase, and towards evening we were invaded in our hotel by the whole troop, every man of them with a more or less mangy cur in his arms, which he tried to persuade me was my lost dog. The more I denied, the more solemnly they insisted, one of them actually going down on his knees, snatching from his bosom an old corroded metal image of the Virgin, and swearing a solemn oath that the Queen of Heaven herself had kindly appeared to him to point out the right animal.

The tumult had increased to such an extent that it looked as if Ralph's disappearance was going to be the cause of a small riot, and finally our landlord had to send for a couple of *Kavasses* from the nearest police station, and have this regiment of bipeds and quadrupeds expelled by main force. I began to be convinced that I should never see my dog again, and I was the more despondent since the porter of the hotel, a semi-respectable old brigand, who, to judge by appearances, had not passed more than half-a-dozen years at the galleys, gravely assured me that all my pains were useless, as my spaniel was undoubtedly dead and devoured too by this time, the Turkish dogs being very fond of their more toothsome English brothers.

All this discussion had taken place in the street at the door of the hotel, and I was about to give up the search for that night at least, and enter the hotel, when an old Greek lady, a Phanariote who had been hearing the fracas from the steps of a door close by, approached our disconsolate group and suggested to Miss H——, one of our party, that we should inquire of the *dervishes* concerning the fate of Ralph.

"And what can the *dervishes* know about my dog?" said I, in no mood to joke, ridiculous as the proposition appeared.

"The holy men know all, *Kyrea* (Madam)," said she, somewhat mysteriously. "Last week I was robbed of my new satin *pelisse*, that my son had just brought me from Broussa, and, as you all see, I have recovered it and have it on my back now."

"Indeed? Then the holy men have also managed to metamorphose your new *pelisse* into an old one by all appearances," said one of the gentlemen who accompanied us, pointing as he spoke to a large rent in the back, which had been clumsily repaired with pins.

"And that is just the most wonderful part of the whole story," quietly answered the *Phanariote*, not in the least disconcerted. "They showed me in the shining circle the quarter of the town, the house, and even the room in which the Jew who had stolen my *pelisse* was just about to rip it up and cut it into pieces. My son and I had barely time to run over to the *Kalindjikoulosek* quarter, and to save my property. We caught the thief in the very act, and we both recognised him as the man shown to us by the *dervishes* in the magic moon. He confessed the theft and is now in prison."

Although none of us had the least comprehension of what she meant by the magic moon and the shining circle, and were all thoroughly mystified by her account of the divining powers of the "holy men," we still felt somehow satisfied from her manner that the story was not altogether a fabrication, and since she had at all events apparently succeeded in recovering her property through being somehow assisted by the *dervishes*, we determined to go the following morning and see for ourselves, for what had helped her might help us likewise.

The monotonous cry of the *Muezzins* from the tops of the minarets had just proclaimed the hour of noon as we, descending from the heights of Pera to the port of Galata, with difficulty managed to elbow our way through the unsavoury crowds of the commercial quarter of the town. Before we reached the docks we had been half deafened by the shouts and incessant ear-piercing cries and the Babel-like confusion of tongues. In this part of the city it is useless to expect to be guided by either house numbers, or names of streets. The location of any desired place is indicated by its proximity to some other more conspicuous building, such as a mosque, bath or European shop; for the rest, one has to trust to *Allah* and his prophet.

It was with the greatest difficulty, therefore, that we finally discovered the British ship-chandler's store, at the rear of which we were to find the place of our destination. Our hotel guide was as ignorant of the *dervishes'* abode as we were ourselves; but at last a small Greek, in all the simplicity of primitive undress, consented for a modest copper *baksheesh* to lead us to the dancers.

When we arrived we were shown into a vast and gloomy hall that looked like a deserted stable. It was long and narrow, the floor was thickly strewn with sand as in a riding school, and it was lighted only by small windows placed at some height from the ground. The *dervishes* had finished their morning performances, and were evidently resting from their exhausting labours. They looked completely prostrated, some lying about in corners, others sitting on their heels staring vacantly into space, engaged, as we were informed, in meditation on their invisible deity. They appeared to have lost all power of sight and hearing, for none of them responded to our questions until a great gaunt figure, wearing a tall cap that made him look at least seven feet high, emerged from an obscure corner. Informing us that he was their chief, the giant gave us to understand that the saintly brethren, being in the habit of receiving orders for additional ceremonies from *Allah* himself, must on no account be disturbed.

But when our interpreter had explained to him the object of our visit, which concerned himself alone, as he was the sole custodian of the "divining rod," his objections vanished and he extended his hand for alms. Upon being gratified, he intimated that only two of our party could be admitted at one time into the confidence of the future, and led the way, followed by Miss

74

H—— and myself.

Plunging after him into what seemed to be a half subterranean passage, we were led to the foot of a tall ladder leading to a chamber under the roof. We scrambled up after our guide, and at the top we found ourselves in a wretched garret of moderate size, with bare walls and destitute of furniture. The floor was carpeted with a thick layer of dust, and cobwebs festooned the walls in neglected confusion. In the corner we saw something that I at first mistook for a bundle of old rags; but the heap presently moved and got on its legs, advanced to the middle of the room and stood before us, the most extraordinary looking creature that I ever beheld. Its sex was female, but whether she was a woman or child it was impossible to decide.

She was a hideous-looking dwarf, with an enormous head, the shoulders of a grenadier, with a waist in proportion; the whole supported by two short, lean, spider-like legs that seemed unequal to the task of bearing the weight of the monstrous body. She had a grinning countenance like the face of a satyr, and it was ornamented with letters and signs from the Koran painted in bright yellow. On her forehead was a blood-red crescent; her head was crowned with a dusty *tarbouche*, or *fez*; her legs were arrayed in large Turkish trousers, and some dirty white muslin wrapped round her body barely sufficed to conceal its hideous deformities. This creature rather let herself drop than sat down in the middle of the floor, and as her weight descended on the rickety boards it sent up a cloud of dust that set us coughing and sneezing. This was the famous Tatmos known as the Damascus oracle!

Without losing time in idle talk, the *dervish* produced a piece of chalk, and traced around the girl a circle about six feet in diameter. Fetching from behind the door twelve small copper lamps which he filled with some dark liquid from a small bottle which he drew from his bosom, he placed them symmetrically around the magic circle. He then broke a chip of wood from a panel of the half ruined door, which bore the marks of many a similar depredation, and, holding the chip between his thumb and finger he began blowing on it at regular intervals, alternating the blowing with mutterings of some kind of weird incantation, till suddenly, and without any apparent cause for its ignition, there appeared a spark on the chip and it blazed up like a dry match. The *dervish* then lit the twelve lamps at this self-generated flame.

During this process, Tatmos, who had sat till then altogether unconcerned and motionless, removed her yellow slippers from her naked feet, and throwing them into a corner, disclosed as an additional beauty, a sixth toe on each deformed foot. The *dervish* now reached over into the circle and seizing the dwarf's ankles gave her a jerk, as if he had been lifting a bag of corn, and raised her clear off the ground, then, stepping back a pace, held her head downward. He shook her as one might a sack to pack its contents, the motion being regular and easy. He then swung her to and fro like a pendulum until the necessary momentum was acquired, when letting go one foot, and seizing the other with both hands, he made a powerful muscular effort and whirled her round in the air as if she had been an Indian club.

My companion had shrunk back in alarm to the farthest corner. Round and round the *dervish* swung his living burden, she remaining perfectly passive. The motion increased in rapidity until the eye could hardly follow the body in its circuit. This continued for perhaps two or three minutes, until, gradually slackening the motion, he at length stopped it altogether, and in an instant had landed the girl on her knees in the middle of the lamp-lit circle. Such was the Eastern mode of mesmerisation as practised among the *dervishes*.

And now the dwarf seemed entirely oblivious of external objects and in a deep trance. Her head and jaw dropped on her chest, her eyes were glazed and staring, and altogether her appearance was even more hideous than before. The *dervish* then carefully closed the shutters of the only window, and we should have been in total obscurity, but that there was a hole bored in it, through which entered a bright ray of sunlight that shot through the darkened room and shone upon the girl. He arranged her drooping head so that the ray should fall upon the crown, after which motioning us to remain silent, he folded his arms upon his bosom, and, fixing his gaze upon the bright spot, became as motionless as a stone image. I, too, riveted my eyes on the same spot, wondering what was to happen next, and how all this strange ceremony was to help me to find Ralph.

By degrees, the bright patch, as if it had drawn through the sunbeam a greater splendour from without and condensed it within its own area, shaped itself into a brilliant star, sending out rays in every direction as from a focus.

A curious optical effect then occurred: the room, which had been previously partially lighted by the sunbeam, grew darker and darker as the star increased in radiance, until we found ourselves in an Egyptian gloom. The star twinkled, trembled and turned, at first with a slow gyratory motion, then faster and faster, increasing its circumference at every rotation until it formed a brilliant disk, and we no longer saw the dwarf, who seemed absorbed into its light. Having gradually attained an extremely rapid velocity, as the girl had done when whirled by the *dervish*, the motion began to decrease and finally merged into a feeble vibration, like the shimmer of moonbeams on rippling water. Then it flickered for a moment longer, emitted a few last flashes, and assuming the density and iridescence of an immense opal, it remained motionless. The disk now radiated a moon-like lustre, soft and silvery, but instead of illuminating the garret, it seemed only to intensify the darkness. The edge of the circle was not *penumbras*, but on the contrary sharply defined like that of a silver shield.

All being now ready, the *dervish* without uttering a word, or removing his gaze from the disk, stretched out a hand, and taking hold of mine, he drew me to his side and pointed to the luminous shield. Looking at the place indicated, we saw large patches appear like those on the moon. These gradually formed themselves into figures that began moving about in high relief in their natural colours. They neither appeared like a photograph nor an engraving; still less like the reflection of images on a mirror, but as if the disk were a cameo, and they were raised above its surface and then endowed with life and motion. To my astonishment and my friend's consternation, we recognised the bridge leading from Galata to Stamboul spanning the Golden Horn from the new to the old city.

There were the people hurrying to and fro, steamers and gay *caiques* gliding on the blue Bosphorus, the many coloured buildings, villas and palaces reflected in the water; and the whole picture illuminated by the noon-day sun. It passed like a panorama, but so vivid was the impression that we could not tell whether it or ourselves were in motion. All was bustle and life, but not a sound broke the oppressive stillness. It was noiseless as a dream. It was a phantom picture. Street after street and quarter after quarter succeeded one another; there was the bazaar, with its narrow, roofed passages, the small shops on either side, the coffee houses with gravely smoking Turks; and as either they glided past us or we past them, one of the smokers upset the *narghilé* and coffee of another, and a volley of soundless invectives caused us great amusement.

So we travelled with the picture until we came to a large building that I recognised as the palace of the Minister of Finance. In a ditch behind the house, and close to a mosque, lying in a pool of mud with his silken coat all bedraggled, lay my poor Ralph! Panting and crouching down as if exhausted, he seemed to be in a dying condition; and near him were gathered some sorry-looking curs who lay blinking in the sun and snapping at the flies!

I had seen all that I desired, although I had not breathed a word about the dog to the *dervish*, and had come more out of curiosity than with the idea of any success. I was impatient to leave at once and recover Ralph, but as my companion besought me to remain a little while longer, I reluctantly consented. The scene faded away and Miss H—— placed herself in turn by the side of the *dervish*.

"I will think of *him*," she whispered in my ear with the eager tone that young ladies generally assume when talking of the worshipped *him*.

There is a long stretch of sand and a blue sea with white waves dancing in the sun, and a great steamer is ploughing her way along past a desolate shore, leaving a milky track behind her. The deck is full of life, the men are busy forward, the cook with white cap and apron is coming out of the galley, uniformed officers are moving about, passengers fill the quarter-deck, lounging, flirting or reading, and a young man we both recognise comes forward and leans over the taffrail. It is—*him*.

Miss H—— gives a little gasp, blushes and smiles, and concentrates her thoughts again. The picture of the steamer vanishes; the magic moon remains for a few moments blank. But new spots appear on its luminous face, we see a library slowly emerging from its depths—a library with green carpet and hangings, and book-shelves round the sides of the room. Seated in an armchair at a table under a hanging lamp, is an old gentleman writing. His gray hair is brushed back from his forehead, his face is smooth-shaven and his countenance has an expression of benignity.

The *dervish* made an hasty motion to enjoin silence; the light on the disk quivers, but resumes its steady brilliancy, and again its surface is imageless for a second.

We are back in Constantinople now and out of the pearly depths of the shield forms our own apartment in the hotel. There are our papers and books on the bureau, my friend's travelling hat in a corner, her ribbons hanging on the glass, and lying on the bed the very dress she had changed when starting out on our expedition. No detail was lacking to make the identification complete; and as if to prove that we were not seeing something conjured up in our own imagination, there lay upon the dressing-table two unopened letters, the handwriting on which was clearly recognised by my friend. They were from a very dear relative of hers, from whom she had expected to hear when in Athens, but had been disappointed.

The scene faded away and we now saw her brother's room with himself lying upon the lounge, and a servant bathing his head, whence, to our horror, blood was trickling. We had left the boy in perfect health but an hour before; and upon seeing this picture my companion uttered a cry of alarm, and seizing me by the hand dragged me to the door. We rejoined our guide and friends in the long hall and hurried back to the hotel.

Young H—— had fallen downstairs and cut his forehead rather badly; in our room, on the dressing-table were the two letters which had arrived in our absence. They had been forwarded from Athens. Ordering a carriage, I at once drove to the Ministry of Finance, and alighting with the guide, hurriedly made for the ditch I had seen for the first time in the shining disk! In the middle of the pool, badly mangled, half-famished, but still alive, lay my beautiful spaniel Ralph, and near him were the blinking curs, unconcernedly snapping at the flies.

From the Polar Lands

(A Christmas Story)

Just a year ago, during the Christmas holidays, a numerous society had gathered in the country house, or rather the old hereditary castle, of a wealthy landowner in Finland. Many were the remains in it of our forefathers' hospitable way of living; and many the medieval customs preserved, founded on traditions and superstitions, semi-Finnish and semi-Russian, the latter imported into it by its female proprietors from the shores of the Neva. Christmas trees were being prepared and implements for divination were being made ready. For, in that old castle there were grim worm-eaten portraits of famous ancestors and knights and ladies, old deserted turrets, with bastions and Gothic windows; mysterious sombre alleys, and dark and endless cellars, easily transformed into subterranean passages and caves, ghostly prison cells, haunted by the restless phantoms of the heroes of local legends. In short, the old manor offered every commodity for romantic horrors. But alas! this once they serve for nought; in the present narrative these dear old horrors play no such part as they otherwise might.

Its chief hero is a very commonplace, prosaical man—let us call him Erkler. Yes; Dr. Erkler, professor of medicine, half-German through his father, a full-blown Russian on his mother's side and by education; and one who looked a rather heavily built, and ordinary mortal. Nevertheless, very extraordinary things happened with him.

Erkler, as it turned out was a great traveller, who by his own choice had accompanied one of the most famous explorers on his journeys round the world. More than once they had both seen death face to face from sunstrokes under the Tropics, from cold in the Polar Regions. All this notwithstanding, the doctor spoke with a never-abating enthusiasm about their "winterings" in Greenland and Novaya Zemla, and about the desert plains in Australia, where he lunched off a kangaroo and dined off an emu, and almost perished of thirst during the passage through a waterless track, which it took them forty hours to cross.

"Yes," he used to remark, "I have experienced almost everything, save what you would describe as *supernatural*. . . . This, of course if we throw out of account a certain extraordinary event in my life—a man I met, of whom I will tell you just now—and its . . . . indeed, rather strange, I may add quite *inexplicable*, results."

There was a loud demand that he should explain himself; and the doctor, forced to yield, began his narrative.

"In 1878 we were compelled to winter on the north-western coast of Spitsbergen. We had been attempting to find our way during the short summer to the pole; but, as usual, the attempt had proved a failure, owing to the icebergs, and, after several such fruitless endeavours, we had to give it up. No sooner had we settled than the polar night descended upon us, our steamers got wedged in and frozen between the blocks of ice in the Gulf of Mussel, and we found ourselves cut off for eight long months from the rest of the living world. . . . I confess I, for one, felt it terribly at first. We became especially discouraged when one stormy night the snow hurricane scattered a mass of materials prepared for our winter buildings, and deprived us of over forty deer from our herd.

"Starvation in prospect is no incentive to good humour; and with the deer we had lost the best *plat de résistance* against polar frosts, human organisms demanding in that climate an increase of heating and solid food. However, we were finally reconciled to our loss, and even got accustomed to the local and in reality more nutritious food—seals, and seal-grease. Our men from the remnants of our lumber built a house neatly divided into two compartments, one for our three professors and myself, and the other for themselves; and, a few wooden sheds being constructed for meteorological, astronomical and magnetic purposes, we even added a protecting stable for the few remaining deer. And then began the monotonous series of dawnless nights and days, hardly distinguishable one from the other, except through dark-gray shadows.

"At times, the 'blues' we got into were fearful! We had contemplated sending two of our three steamers home in September, but the premature and unforeseen formation of ice walls round them had thwarted our plans; and now, with the entire crews on our hands, we had to economize still more with our meagre provisions, fuel and light. Lamps were used only for scientific purposes: the rest of the time we had to content ourselves with God's light—the moon and the *Aurora Borealis*. . . . But how describe these glorious, incomparable northern lights! Rings, arrows, gigantic conflagrations of accurately divided rays of the most vivid and varied colours. The November moonlight nights were as gorgeous. The play of moonbeams on the snow and the frozen rocks was most striking. These were fairy nights.

"Well, one such night—it may have been one such *day*, for all I know, as from the end of November to about the middle of March we had no twilights at all, to distinguish the one from the other—we suddenly espied in the play of coloured beams, which were then throwing a golden rosy hue on the snow plains, a dark moving spot. . . . It grew, and seemed to scatter as it approached nearer to us. What did this mean? . . . . It looked like a herd of cattle, or a group of living men, trotting over the snowy wilderness. . . . But animals there were white like everything else. What then was this?. . . . . human beings? . . . .

"We could not believe our eyes. Yes, a group of men was approaching our dwelling. It turned out to be about fifty seal-hunters, guided by Matiliss, a well-known veteran mariner, from Norway. They had been caught by the icebergs, just as we had been.

"'How did you know that we were here?' we asked.

"'Old Johan, this very same old party, showed us the way'—they answered, pointing to a venerable-looking old man with snow-white locks.

"In sober truth, it would have beseemed their guide far better to have sat at home over his fire than to have been seal-hunting in polar lands with younger men. And we told them so, still wondering how he came to learn of our presence in this kingdom of white bears. At this Matiliss and his companions smiled, assuring us that 'old Johan' *knew all*. They remarked that we must be novices in polar borderlands, since we were ignorant of Johan's personality and could still wonder at anything said of him.

"'It is nigh forty-five years,' said the chief hunter, 'that I have been catching seals in the Polar Seas, and as far as my personal remembrance goes, I have always known him, and just as he is now, an old, white-bearded man. And so far back as in the days when I used to go to sea, as a small boy with my father, my dad used to tell me the same of old Johan, and he added that his own father and grandfather too, had known Johan in their days of boyhood, none of them having ever seen him otherwise than white as our snows. And, as our forefathers nicknamed him "the white-haired all-knower," thus do we, the seal hunters, call him, to this day.'

"'Would you make us believe he is two hundred years old?'—we laughed.

"Some of our sailors crowding round the white-haired phenomenon, plied him with questions.

"'Grandfather! answer us, how old are you?'

"'I really do not know it myself, sonnies. I live as long as God has decreed me to. As to my years, I never counted them.'

"'And how did you know, grandfather, that we were wintering in this place?'

"'God guided me. How I learned it I do not know; save that I knew—I knew it.'"

The Ensouled Violin

1

In the year 1828, an old German, a music teacher, came to Paris with his pupil and settled unostentatiously in one of the quiet *faubourgs* of the metropolis. The first rejoiced in the name of Samuel Klaus; the second answered to the more poetical appellation of Franz Stenio. The younger man was a violinist, gifted, as rumour went, with extraordinary, almost miraculous talent. Yet as he was poor and had not hitherto made a name for himself in Europe, he remained for several years in the capital of France—the heart and pulse of capricious continental fashion—unknown and unappreciated. Franz was a Styrian by birth, and, at the time of the event to be presently described, he was a young man considerably under thirty.

A philosopher and a dreamer by nature, imbued with all the mystic oddities of true genius, he reminded one of some of the heroes in Hoffmann's *Contes Fantastiques*. His earlier existence had been a very unusual, in fact, quite an eccentric one, and its history must be briefly told—for the better understanding of the present story.

Born of very pious country people, in a quiet burg among the Styrian Alps; nursed "by the native gnomes who watched over his cradle"; growing up in the weird atmosphere of the ghouls and vampires who play such a prominent part in the household of every Styrian and Slavonian in Southern Austria; educated later, as a student, in the shadow of the old Rhenish castles of Germany; Franz from his childhood had passed through every emotional stage on the plane of the so-called "supernatural." He had also studied at one time the "occult arts" with an enthusiastic disciple of Paracelsus and Kunrath; alchemy had few theoretical secrets for him; and he had dabbled in "ceremonial magic" and "sorcery" with some Hungarian Tziganes. Yet he loved above all else music, and above music—his violin.

At the age of twenty-two he suddenly gave up his practical studies in the occult, and from that day, though as devoted as ever in thought to the beautiful Grecian Gods, he surrendered himself entirely to his art. Of his classic studies he had retained only that which related to the muses—Euterpe especially, at whose altar he worshipped—and Orpheus whose magic lyre he tried to emulate with his violin. Except his dreamy belief in the nymphs and the sirens, on account probably of the double relationship of the latter to the muses through Calliope and Orpheus, he was interested but little in the matters of this sublunary world. All his aspirations mounted, like incense, with the wave of the heavenly harmony that he drew from his instrument, to a higher and a nobler sphere. He dreamed awake, and lived a real though an enchanted life only during those hours when his magic bow carried him along the wave of sound to the Pagan Olympus, to the feet of Euterpe.

A strange child he had ever been in his own home, where tales of magic and witchcraft grow out of every inch of the soil; a still stranger boy he had become, until finally he had blossomed into manhood, without one single characteristic of youth. Never had a fair face attracted his attention; not for one moment had his thoughts turned from his solitary studies to a life beyond that of a mystic Bohemian. Content with his own company, he had thus passed the best years of his youth and manhood with his violin for his chief idol, and with the Gods and Goddesses of old Greece for his audience, in perfect ignorance of practical life. His whole existence had been one long day of dreams, of melody and sunlight, and he had never felt any other aspirations.

How useless, but oh, how glorious those dreams! how vivid! and why should he desire any better fate? Was he not all that he wanted to be, transformed in a second of thought into one or another hero; from Orpheus, who held all nature breathless, to the urchin who piped away under the plane tree to the *naiads* of Callirrhoe's crystal fountain? Did not the swift-footed nymphs frolic at his beck and call to the sound of the magic flute of the Arcadian Shepherd—who was himself? Behold, the Goddess of Love and Beauty herself descending from on high, attracted by the sweet-voiced notes of his violin! . . .

Yet there came a time when he preferred Syrinx to Aphrodite—not as the fair nymph pursued by Pan, but after her transformation by the merciful Gods into the reed out of which the frustrated God of the Shepherds had made his magic pipe. For also, with time, ambition grows and is rarely satisfied. When he tried to emulate on his violin the enchanting sounds that resounded in his mind, the whole of Parnassus kept silent under the spell, or joined in heavenly chorus; but the audience he finally craved was composed of more than the Gods sung by Hesiod, verily of the most appreciative *mélomanes* of European capitals. He felt jealous of the magic pipe, and would fain have had it at his command.

"Oh, that I could allure a nymph into my beloved violin!"— he often cried, after awakening from one of his daydreams. "Oh, that I could only span in spirit flight the abyss of Time! Oh, that I could find myself for one short day a partaker of the secret arts of the Gods, a God myself, in the sight and hearing of enraptured humanity; and, having learned the mystery of the lyre of Orpheus, or secured within my violin a siren, thereby benefit mortals to my own glory!"

Thus, having for long years dreamed in the company of the Gods of his fancy, he now took to dreaming of the transitory glories of fame upon this earth. But at this time he was suddenly called home by his widowed mother from one of the German universities where he had lived for the last year or two. This was an event which brought his plans to an end, at least so far as the immediate future was concerned, for he had hitherto drawn upon her alone for his meagre pittance, and his means were not sufficient for an independent life outside his native place.

His return had a very unexpected result. His mother, whose only love he was on earth, died soon after she had welcomed her Benjamin back; and the good wives of the burg exercised their swift tongues for many a month after as to the real causes of that death.

Frau Stenio, before Franz's return, was a healthy, buxom, middle-aged body, strong and hearty. She was a pious and a God-fearing soul too, who had never failed in saying her prayers, nor had missed an early mass for years during his absence. On the first Sunday after her son had settled at home—a day that she had been longing for and had anticipated for months in joyous visions, in which she saw him kneeling by her side in the little church on the hill—she called him from the foot of the stairs. The hour had come when her pious dream was to be realised, and she was waiting for him, carefully wiping the dust from the prayer-book he had used in his boyhood.

But instead of Franz, it was his violin that responded to her call, mixing its sonorous voice with the rather cracked tones of the peal of the merry Sunday bells. The fond mother was somewhat shocked at hearing the prayer-inspiring sounds drowned by the weird, fantastic notes of the "Dance of the Witches"; they seemed to her so unearthly and mocking. But she almost fainted upon hearing the definite refusal of her well-beloved son to go to church. He never went to church, he coolly remarked. It was loss of time; besides which, the loud peals of the old church organ jarred on his nerves. Nothing should induce him to submit to the torture of listening to that cracked organ. He was firm and nothing could move him. To her supplications and remonstrances he put an end by offering to play for her a "Hymn to the Sun" he had just composed.

From that memorable Sunday morning, Frau Stenio lost her usual serenity of mind. She hastened to lay her sorrows and seek for consolation at the foot of the confessional; but that which she heard in response from the stern priest filled her gentle and unsophisticated soul with dismay and almost with despair. A feeling of fear, a sense of profound terror, which soon became a chronic state with her, pursued her from that moment; her nights became disturbed and sleepless, her days passed in prayer and lamentations. In her maternal anxiety for the salvation of her beloved son's soul, and for his *post-mortem* welfare, she made a series of rash vows.

Finding that neither the Latin petition to the Mother of God written for her by her spiritual adviser, nor yet the humble supplications in German, addressed by herself to every saint she had reason to believe was residing in Paradise, worked the desired effect, she took to pilgrimages to distant shrines. During one of these journeys to a holy chapel situated high up in the mountains, she caught cold, amidst the glaciers of the Tyrol, and redescended only to take to a sick bed, from which she arose no more. Frau Stenio's vow had led her, in one sense, to the desired result. The poor woman was now given an opportunity of seeking out in *propria persona* the saints she had believed in so well, and of pleading face to face for the recreant son, who refused adherence to them and to the Church, scoffed at monk and confessional, and held the organ in such horror.

Franz sincerely lamented his mother's death. Unaware of being the indirect cause of it, he felt no remorse; but selling the modest household goods and chattels, light in purse and heart, he resolved to travel on foot for a year or two, before settling down to any definite profession.

A hazy desire to see the great cities of Europe, and to try his luck in France, lurked at the bottom of this travelling project, but his Bohemian habits of life were too strong to be abruptly abandoned. He placed his small capital with a banker for a rainy day, and started on his pedestrian journey *via* Germany and Austria. His violin paid for his board and lodging in the inns and farms on his way, and he passed his days in the green fields and in the solemn silent woods, face to face with Nature, dreaming all the time as usual with his eyes open. During the three months of his pleasant travels to and fro, he never descended for one moment from Parnassus; but, as an alchemist transmutes lead into gold, so he transformed everything on his way into a song of Hesiod or Anacreon. Every evening, while fiddling for his supper and bed, whether on a green lawn or in the hall of a rustic inn, his fancy changed the whole scene for him.

Village swains and maidens became transfigured into Arcadian shepherds and nymphs. The sand-covered floor was now a green sward; the uncouth couples spinning round in a measured waltz with the wild grace of tamed bears became priests and priestesses of Terpsichore; the bulky, cherry-cheeked and blue-eyed daughters of rural Germany were the Hesperides circling around the trees laden with the golden apples. Nor did the melodious strains of the Arcadian demi-gods piping on their *syrinxes*, and audible but to his own enchanted ear, vanish with the dawn. For no sooner was the curtain of sleep raised from his eyes than he would sally forth into a new magic realm of daydreams.

On his way to some dark and solemn pine-forest, he played incessantly, to himself and to everything else. He fiddled to the green hill, and forthwith the mountain and the moss-covered rocks moved forward to hear him the better, as they had done at the sound of the Orphean lyre. He fiddled to the merry-voiced brook, to the hurrying river, and both slackened their speed and stopped their waves, and, becoming silent, seemed to listen to him in an entranced rapture. Even the long-legged stork who stood meditatively on one leg on the thatched top of the rustic mill, gravely resolving unto himself the problem of his too-long existence, sent out after him a long and strident cry, screeching, "Art thou Orpheus himself, O Stenio?"

It was a period of full bliss, of a daily and almost hourly exaltation. The last words of his dying mother, whispering to him of the horrors of eternal condemnation, had left him unaffected, and the only vision her warning evoked in him was that of Pluto. By a ready association of ideas, he saw the lord of the dark nether kingdom greeting him as he had greeted the husband of Eurydice before him. Charmed with the magic sounds of his violin, the wheel of Ixion was at a standstill once more, thus affording relief to the wretched seducer of Juno, and giving the lie to those who claim eternity for the duration of the punishment of condemned sinners.

He perceived Tantalus forgetting his never-ceasing thirst, and smacking his lips as he drank in the heaven-born melody; the stone of Sisyphus becoming motionless, the Furies themselves smiling on him, and the sovereign of the gloomy regions delighted, and awarding preference to his violin over the lyre of Orpheus. Taken *au sérieux,* mythology thus seems a decided antidote to fear, in the face of theological threats, especially when strengthened with an insane and passionate love of music; with Franz, Euterpe proved always victorious in every contest, aye, even with Hell itself!

But there is an end to everything, and very soon Franz had to give up uninterrupted dreaming. He had reached the university town where dwelt his old violin teacher, Samuel Klaus. When this antiquated musician found that his beloved and favourite pupil, Franz, had been left poor in purse and still poorer in earthly affections, he felt his strong attachment to the boy awaken with tenfold force. He took Franz to his heart, and forthwith adopted him as his son.

The old teacher reminded people of one of those grotesque figures which look as if they had just stepped out of some medieval panel. And yet Klaus, with his fantastic *allures* of a night-goblin, had the most loving heart, as tender as that of a woman, and the self-sacrificing nature of an old Christian martyr. When Franz had briefly narrated to him the history of his last few years, the professor took him by the hand, and leading him into his study simply said:

"Stop with me, and put an end to your Bohemian life. Make yourself famous. I am old and childless and will be your father. Let us live together and forget all save fame."

And forthwith he offered to proceed with Franz to Paris, *via* several large German cities, where they would stop to give concerts.

In a few days Klaus succeeded in making Franz forget his vagrant life and its artistic independence, and reawakened in his pupil his now dormant ambition and desire for worldly fame. Hitherto, since his mother's death, he had been content to received applause only from the Gods and Goddesses who inhabited his vivid fancy; now he began to crave once more for the admiration of mortals.

Under the clever and careful training of old Klaus his remarkable talent gained in strength and powerful charm with every day, and his reputation grew and expanded with every city and town wherein he made himself heard. His ambition was being rapidly realised; the presiding *genii* of various musical centres to whose patronage his talent was submitted soon proclaimed him *the one* violinist of the day, and the public declared loudly that he stood unrivalled by any one whom they had ever heard. These laudations very soon made both master and pupil completely lose their heads.

But Paris was less ready with such appreciation. Paris makes reputations for itself, and will take none on faith. They had been living in it for almost three years, and were still climbing with difficulty the artist's Calvary, when an event occurred which put an end even to their most modest expectations. The first arrival of Niccolo Paganini was suddenly heralded, and threw Lutetia into a convulsion of expectation. The unparalleled artist arrived, and—all Paris fell at once at his feet.

2

Now it is a well known fact that a superstition born in the dark days of medieval superstition, and surviving almost to the middle of the present century, attributed all such abnormal, out-of-the-way talent as that of Paganini to "supernatural" agency. Every great and marvellous artist had been accused in his day of dealings with the devil. A few instances will suffice to refresh the reader's memory.

Tartini, the great composer and violinist of the seventeenth century, was denounced as one who got his best inspirations from the Evil One, with whom he was, it was said, in regular league. This accusation was, of course, due to the almost magical impression he produced upon his audiences. His inspired performance on the violin secured for him in his native country the title of "Master of Nations."

The *Sonate du Diable*, also called "Tartini's Dream"—as everyone who has heard it will be ready to testify—is the most weird melody ever heard or invented: hence, the marvellous composition has become the source of endless legends. Nor were they entirely baseless, since it was he, himself, who was shown to have originated them. Tartini confessed to having written it on awakening from a dream, in which he had heard his *sonata* performed by Satan, for his benefit, and in consequence of a bargain made with his infernal majesty.

Several famous singers, even, whose exceptional voices struck the hearers with superstitious admiration, have not escaped a like accusation. Pasta's splendid voice was attributed in her day to the fact that, three months before her birth, the diva's mother was carried during a trance to heaven, and there treated to a vocal concert of seraphs. Malibran was indebted for her voice to St. Cecelia, while others said she owed it to a demon who watched over her cradle and sung the baby to sleep. Finally, Paganini—the unrivalled performer, the mean Italian, who like Dryden's Jubal striking on the "chorded shell" forced the throngs that followed him to worship the divine sounds produced, and made people say that "less than a God could not dwell within the hollow of his violin"—Paganini left a legend too.

The almost supernatural art of the greatest violin player that the world has ever known was often speculated upon, never understood. The effect produced by him on his audience was literally marvellous, overpowering. The great Rossini is said to have wept like a sentimental German maiden on hearing him play for the first time. The Princess Elisa of Lucca, a sister of the great Napoleon, in whose service Paganini was, as director of her private orchestra, for a long time was unable to hear him play without fainting. In women he produced nervous fits and hysterics at his will; stout-hearted men he drove to frenzy. He changed cowards into heroes and made the bravest soldiers feel like so many nervous school-girls.

Is it to be wondered at, then, that hundreds of weird tales circulated for long years about and around the mysterious Genoese, that modern Orpheus of Europe? One of these was especially ghastly. It was rumoured, and was believed by more people than would probably like to confess it, that the strings of his violin were made of *human intestines, according to all the rules and requirements of the Black Art.*

Exaggerated as this idea may seem to some, it has nothing impossible in it; and it is more than probable that it was this legend that led to the extraordinary events which we are about to narrate. Human organs are often used by the Eastern Black Magician, so-called, and it is an averred fact that some Bengâlî *Tântrikas* (reciters of *tantras*, or "invocations to the demon," as a reverend writer has described them) use human corpses, and certain internal and external organs pertaining to them, as powerful magical agents for bad purposes.

However this may be, now that the magnetic and mesmeric potencies of hypnotism are recognised as facts by most physicians, it may be suggested with less danger than heretofore that the extraordinary effects of Paganini's violin-playing were not, perhaps, entirely due to his talent and genius. The wonder and awe he so easily excited were as much caused by his external appearance, "which had something weird and demoniacal in it," according to certain of his biographers, as by the inexpressible charm of his execution and his remarkable mechanical skill. The latter is demonstrated by his perfect imitation of the *flageolet,* and his performance of long and magnificent melodies on the G string alone. In this performance, which many an artist has tried to copy without success, he remains unrivalled to this day.

It is owing to this remarkable appearance of his—termed by his friends eccentric, and by his too nervous victims, diabolical—that he experienced great difficulties in refuting certain ugly rumors. These were credited far more easily in his day than they would be now. It was whispered throughout Italy, and even in his own native town, that Paganini had murdered his wife, and, later on, a mistress, both of whom he had loved passionately, and both of whom he had not hesitated to sacrifice to his fiendish ambition. He had made himself proficient in magic arts, it was asserted, and had succeeded thereby in imprisoning the souls of his two victims in his violin—his famous Cremona.

It is maintained by the immediate friends of Ernst T. W. Hoffmann, the celebrated author of *Die Elixire des Teufels*, *Meister Martin*, and other charming and mystical tales, that Councillor Crespel, in the *Violin of Cremona*, was taken from the legend about Paganini. It is, as all who have read it know, the history of a celebrated violin, into which the voice and the soul of a famous diva, a woman whom Crespel had loved and killed, had passed, and to which was added the voice of his beloved daughter, Antonia.

Nor was this superstition utterly ungrounded, nor was Hoffmann to be blamed for adopting it, after he had heard Paganini's playing. The extraordinary facility with which the artist drew out of his instrument, not only the most unearthly sounds, but positively human voices, justified the suspicion. Such effects might well have startled an audience and thrown terror into many a nervous heart. Add to this the impenetrable mystery connected with a certain period of Paganini's youth, and the most wild tales about him must be found in a measure justifiable, and even excusable; especially among a nation whose ancestors knew the Borgias and the Medicis of Black Art fame.

3

In those pre-telegraphic days, newspapers were limited, and the wings of fame had a heavier flight than they have now. Franz had hardly heard of Paganini; and when he did, he swore he would rival, if not eclipse, the Genoese magician. Yes, he would either become the most famous of all living violinists, or he would break his instrument and put an end to his life at the same time.

Old Klaus rejoiced at such a determination. He rubbed his hands in glee, and jumping about on his lame leg like a crippled satyr, he flattered and incensed his pupil, believing himself all the while to be performing a sacred duty to the holy and majestic cause of art.

Upon first setting foot in Paris, three years before, Franz had all but failed. Musical critics pronounced him a rising star, but had all agreed that he required a few more years' practice, before he could hope to carry his audiences by storm. Therefore, after a desperate study of over two years and uninterrupted preparations, the Styrian artist had finally made himself ready for his first serious appearance in the great Opera House where a public concert before the most exacting critics of the old world was to be held; at this critical moment Paganini's arrival in the European metropolis placed an obstacle in the way of the realisation of his hopes, and the old German professor wisely postponed his pupil's *début*.

At first he had simply smiled at the wild enthusiasm, the laudatory hymns sung about the Genoese violinist, and the almost superstitious awe with which his name was pronounced. But very soon Paganini's name became a burning iron in the hearts of both the artists, and a threatening phantom in the mind of Klaus. A few days more, and they shuddered at the very mention of their great rival, whose success became with every night more unprecedented.

The first series of concerts was over, but neither Klaus nor Franz had as yet had an opportunity of hearing him and of judging for themselves. So great and so beyond their means was the charge for admission, and so small the hope of getting a free pass from a brother artist justly regarded as the meanest of men in monetary transactions, that they had to wait for a chance, as did so many others. But the day came when neither master nor pupil could control their impatience any longer; so they pawned their watches, and with the proceeds bought two modest seats.

Who can describe the enthusiasm, the triumphs, of this famous, and at the same time fatal night! The audience was frantic; men wept and women screamed and fainted; while both Klaus and Stenio sat looking paler than two ghosts. At the first touch of Paganini's magic bow, both Franz and Samuel felt as if the icy hand of death had touched them. Carried away by an irresistible enthusiasm, which turned into a violent, unearthly mental torture, they dared neither look into each other's faces, nor exchange one word during the whole performance.

At midnight, while the chosen delegates of the Musical Societies and the Conservatory of Paris unhitched the horses, and dragged the carriage of the grand artist home in triumph, the two Germans returned to their modest lodging, and it was a pitiful sight to see them. Mournful and desperate, they placed themselves in their usual seats at the fire-corner, and neither for a while opened his mouth.

"Samuel!" at last exclaimed Franz, pale as death itself. "Samuel—it remains for us now but to die! .... Do you hear me? .... We are worthless! We were two madmen to have ever hoped that anyone in this world would ever rival .... him."

The name of Paganini stuck in his throat, as in utter despair he fell into his arm chair.

The old professor's wrinkles suddenly became purple. His little greenish eyes gleamed phosphorescently as, bending toward his pupil, he whispered to him in hoarse and broken tones:

"*Nein, Nein!* Thou art wrong, my Franz! I have taught thee, and thou hast learned all of the great art that a simple mortal, and a Christian by baptism, can learn from another simple mortal. Am I to blame because these accursed Italians, in order to reign unequalled in the domain of art, have recourse to Satan and the diabolical effects of Black Magic?"

Franz turned his eyes upon his old master. There was a sinister light burning in those glittering orbs; a light telling plainly that, to secure such a power, he, too, would not scruple to sell himself, body and soul, to the Evil One.

But he said not a word, and, turning his eyes from his old master's face, gazed dreamily at the dying embers.

The same long-forgotten incoherent dreams, which, after seeming such realities to him in his younger days, had been given up entirely, and had gradually faded from his mind, now crowded back into it with the same force and vividness as of old. The grimacing shades of Ixion, Sisyphus and Tantalus resurrected and stood before him, saying:

"What matters hell—in which thou believest not. And even if hell there be, it is the hell described by the old Greeks, not that of the modern bigots—a locality full of conscious shadows, to whom thou canst be a second Orpheus."

Franz felt that he was going mad, and, turning instinctively, he looked his old master once more right in the face. Then his bloodshot eye evaded the gaze of Klaus.

Whether Samuel understood the terrible state of mind of his pupil, or whether he wanted to draw him out, to make him speak, and thus to divert his thoughts, must remain as hypothetical to the reader as it is to the writer. Whatever may have been in his mind, the German enthusiast went on, speaking with a feigned calmness:

"Franz, my dear boy, I tell you that the art of the accursed Italian is not natural; that it is due neither to study nor to genius. It never was acquired in the usual, natural way. You need not stare at me in that wild manner, for what I say is in the mouth of millions of people. Listen to what I now tell you, and try to understand. You have heard the strange tale whispered about the famous Tartini? He died one fine Sabbath night strangled by his familiar demon, who had taught him how to endow his violin with a human voice, by shutting up in it, by means of incantations, the soul of a young virgin.

"Paganini did more. In order to endow his instrument with the faculty of emitting human sounds, such as sobs, despairing cries, supplications, moans of love and fury—in short, the most heart-rending notes of the human voice—Paganini became the murderer not only of his wife and his mistress, but also of a friend, who was more tenderly attached to him than any other being on this earth. He then made the four chords of his magic violin out of the intestines of his last victim. This is the secret of his enchanting talent of that overpowering melody, that combination of sounds, which you will never be able to master unless . . . . ."

The old man could not finish his sentence. He staggered back before the fiendish look of his pupil, and covered his face with his hands.

Franz was breathing heavily, and his eyes had an expression which reminded Klaus of those of a hyena. His pallor was cadaverous. For some time he could not speak, but only gasp for breath. At last he slowly muttered:

"Are you in earnest?"

"I am, as I hope to help you."

"And. . . . And do you really believe that had I only the means of obtaining human intestines for strings, I could rival Paganini?" asked Franz, after a moment's pause, and casting down his eyes.

The old German unveiled his face, and, with a strange look of determination upon it, softly answered:

"Human intestines alone are not sufficient for our purpose; they must have belonged to someone who had loved us well, with an unselfish, holy love. Tartini endowed his violin with the life of a virgin; but that virgin had died of unrequited love for him. The fiendish artist had prepared beforehand a tube, in which he managed to catch her last breath as she expired, pronouncing his beloved name, and he then transferred this breath to his violin. As to Paganini, I have just told you his tale. It was with the consent of his victim, though, that he murdered him to get possession of his intestines.

"Oh, for the power of the human voice!" Samuel went on, after a brief pause. "What can equal the eloquence, the magic spell of the human voice? Do you think, my poor boy, I would not have taught you this great, this final secret, were it not that it throws one right into the clutches of him ... who must remain unnamed at night?" he added, with a sudden return to the superstitions of his youth.

Franz did not answer; but with a calmness awful to behold, he left his place, took down his violin from the wall where it was hanging, and, with one powerful grasp of the chords, he tore them out and flung them into the fire.

Samuel suppressed a cry of horror. The chords were hissing

upon the coals, where, among the blazing logs, they wriggled and curled like so many living snakes.

"By the witches of Thessaly and the dark arts of Circe!" he exclaimed, with foaming mouth and his eyes burning like coals; "by the Furies of Hell and Pluto himself, I now swear, in thy presence, O Samuel, my master, never to touch a violin again until I can string it with four human chords. May I be accursed for ever and ever if I do!" He fell senseless on the floor, with a deep sob, that ended like a funeral wail; old Samuel lifted him up as he would have lifted a child, and carried him to his bed. Then he sallied forth in search of a physician.

4

For several days after this painful scene Franz was very ill, ill almost beyond recovery. The physician declared him to be suffering from brain fever and said that the worst was to be feared. For nine long days the patient remained delirious; and Klaus, who was nursing him night and day with the solicitude of the tenderest mother, was horrified at the work of his own hands. For the first time since their acquaintance began, the old teacher, owing to the wild ravings of his pupil, was able to penetrate into the darkest corners of that weird, superstitious, cold, and, at the same time, passionate nature; and—he trembled at what he discovered. For he saw that which he had failed to perceive before—Franz as he was in reality, and not as he seemed to superficial observers.

Music was the life of the young man, and adulation was the air he breathed, without which that life became a burden; from the chords of his violin alone, Stenio drew his life and being, but the applause of men and even of Gods was necessary to its support. He saw unveiled before his eyes a genuine, artistic, *earthly* soul, with its divine counterpart totally absent, a son of the Muses, all fancy and brain poetry, but without a heart. While listening to the ravings of that delirious and unhinged fancy Klaus felt as if he were for the first time in his long life exploring a marvellous and untraveled region, a human nature not of

100

this world but of some incomplete planet. He saw all this, and shuddered. More than once he asked himself whether it would not be doing a kindness to his "boy" to let him die before he returned to consciousness.

But he loved his pupil too well to dwell for long on such an idea. Franz had bewitched his truly artistic nature, and now old Klaus felt as though their two lives were inseparably linked together. That he could thus feel was a revelation to the old man; so he decided to save Franz, even at the expense of his own old and, as he thought, useless life.

The seventh day of the illness brought on a most terrible crisis. For twenty-four hours the patient never closed his eyes, nor remained for a moment silent; he raved continuously during the whole time. His visions were peculiar, and he minutely described each. Fantastic, ghastly figures kept slowly swimming out of the penumbra of his small dark room, in regular and uninterrupted procession, and he greeted each by name as he might greet old acquaintances. He referred to himself as Prometheus, bound to the rock by four bands made of human intestines. At the foot of the Caucasian Mount the black waters of the River Styx were running. . . . They had deserted Arcadia, and were now endeavouring to encircle within a seven-fold embrace the rock upon which he was suffering. . . .

"Wouldst thou know the name of the Promethean rock, old man?" he roared into his adopted father's ear. . . . "Listen then, ... its name is . . . . called . . . . Samuel Klaus. . . . ."

"Yes, yes! . . . ." the German murmured disconsolately. "It is I who killed him, while seeking to console. The news of Paganini's magic arts struck his fancy too vividly. . . . Oh, my poor, poor boy!"

"Ha, ha, ha, ha!" The patient broke into a loud and discordant laugh. "Aye, poor old man, sayest thou? . . . . So, so, thou art of poor stuff, anyhow, and wouldst look well only when stretched upon a fine Cremona violin! . . ."

Klaus shuddered, but said nothing. He only bent over the poor maniac, and with a kiss upon his brow, a caress as tender and as gentle as that of a doting mother, he left the sick-room for a few instants, to seek relief in his own garret. When he returned, the ravings were following another channel. Franz was singing, trying to imitate the sounds of a violin.

Toward the evening of that day, the delirium of the sick man became perfectly ghastly. He saw spirits of fire clutching at his violin. Their skeleton hands, from each finger of which grew a flaming claw, beckoned to old Samuel. . . . They approached and surrounded the old master, and were preparing to rip him open. . . . him "the only man on this earth who loves me with an unselfish, holy love, and. . . . whose intestines can be of any good at all!" he went on whispering, with glaring eyes and demon laugh. . . .

By the next morning, however, the fever had disappeared, and by the end of the ninth day Stenio had left his bed, having no recollection of his illness, and no suspicion that he had allowed Klaus to read his inner thought. Nay; had he himself any knowledge that such a horrible idea as the sacrifice of his old master to his ambition had ever entered his mind? Hardly. The only immediate result of his fatal illness was, that as, by reason of his vow, his artistic passion could find no issue, another passion awoke, which might avail to feed his ambition and his insatiable fancy. He plunged headlong into the study of the Occult Arts, of Alchemy and of Magic. In the practice of Magic the young dreamer sought to stifle the voice of his passionate longing for his, as he thought, for ever lost violin . . . .

Weeks and months passed away, and the conversation about Paganini was never resumed between the master and the pupil. But a profound melancholy had taken possession of Franz, the two hardly exchanged a word, the violin hung mute, chordless, full of dust, in its habitual place. It was as the presence of a soulless corpse between them.

The young man had become gloomy and sarcastic, even avoiding the mention of music. Once, as his old professor, after long hesitation, took out his own violin from its dust-covered case and prepared to play, Franz gave a convulsive shudder, but said nothing. At the first notes of the bow, however, he glared like a madman, and rushing out of the house, remained for hours, wandering in the streets. Then old Samuel in his turn threw his instrument down, and locked himself up in his room till the following morning.

One night as Franz sat, looking particularly pale and gloomy, old Samuel suddenly jumped from his seat, and after hopping about the room in a magpie fashion, approached his pupil, imprinted a fond kiss upon the young man's brow, and squeaked at the top of his shrill voice:

"Is it not time to put an end to all this?" . . . .

Whereupon, starting from his usual lethargy, Franz echoed, as in a dream:

"Yes, it is time to put an end to this."

Upon which the two separated, and went to bed.

On the following morning, when Franz awoke, he was astonished not to see his old teacher in his usual place to greet him. But he had greatly altered during the last few months, and he at first paid no attention to his absence, unusual as it was. He dressed and went into the adjoining room, a little parlour where they had their meals, and which separated their two bedrooms. The fire had not been lighted since the embers had died out on the previous night, and no sign was anywhere visible of the professor's busy hand in his usual housekeeping duties. Greatly puzzled, but in no way dismayed, Franz took his usual place at the corner of the now cold fireplace, and fell into an aimless reverie. As he stretched himself in his old armchair, raising both his hands to clasp them behind his head in a favourite posture of his, his hand came into contact with something on a shelf at his back; he knocked against a case, and brought it violently on the ground.

It was old Klaus' violin-case that came down to the floor with such a sudden crash that the case opened and the violin fell out of it, rolling to the feet of Franz. And then the chords, striking against the brass fender emitted a sound, prolonged, sad and mournful as the sigh of an unrestful soul; it seemed to fill the whole room, and reverberated in the head and the very heart of the young man. The effect of that broken violin-string was magical.

"Samuel!" cried Stenio, with his eyes starting from their sockets, and an unknown terror suddenly taking possession of his whole being. "Samuel! what has happened? . . . . My good, my dear old master!" he called out, hastening to the professor's little room, and throwing the door violently open. No one answered, all was silent within.

He staggered back, frightened at the sound of his own voice, so changed and hoarse it seemed to him at this moment. No reply came in response to his call. Naught followed but a dead silence . . . . that stillness which, in the domain of sounds, usually denotes death. In the presence of a corpse, as in the lugubrious stillness of a tomb, such silence acquires a mysterious power, which strikes the sensitive soul with a nameless terror. . . . The little room was dark, and Franz hastened to open the shutters.

★★★★★★

Samuel was lying on his bed, cold, stiff, and lifeless.... At the sight of the corpse of him who had loved him so well, and had been to him more than a father, Franz experienced a dreadful revulsion of feeling, a terrible shock. But the ambition of the fanatical artist got the better of the despair of the man, and smothered the feelings of the latter in a few seconds.

A note bearing his own name was conspicuously placed upon a table near the corpse. With trembling hand, the violinist tore open the envelope, and read the following:

My Beloved Son, Franz,
When you read this, I shall have made the greatest sacrifice that your best and only friend and teacher could have accomplished for your fame. He, who loved you most, is now but an inanimate lump of clay. Of your old teacher there now remains but a clod of cold organic matter. I need not prompt you as to what you have to do with it. Fear not stupid prejudices. It is for your future fame that

I have made an offering of my body, and you would be guilty of the blackest ingratitude were you now to render useless this sacrifice. When you shall have replaced the chords upon your violin, and these chords a portion of my own self, under your touch it will acquire the power of that accursed sorcerer, all the magic voices of Paganini's instrument.

You will find therein my voice, my sighs and groans, my song of welcome, the prayerful sobs of my infinite and sorrowful sympathy, my love for you. And now, my Franz, fear nobody! Take your instrument with you, and dog the steps of him who filled our lives with bitterness and despair! . . . . Appear in every arena, where, hitherto, he has reigned without a rival, and bravely throw the gauntlet of defiance in his face. O Franz! then only wilt thou hear with what a magic power the full notes of unselfish love will issue forth from thy violin. Perchance, with a last caressing touch of its chords, thou wilt remember that they once formed a portion of thine old teacher, who now embraces and blesses thee for the last time.

Samuel

Two burning tears sparkled in the eyes of Franz, but they dried up instantly. Under the fiery rush of passionate hope and pride, the two orbs of the future magician-artist, riveted to the ghastly face of the dead man, shone like the eyes of a demon.

Our pen refuses to describe that which took place on that day, after the legal inquiry was over. As another note, written with the view of satisfying the authorities, had been prudently provided by the loving care of the old teacher, the verdict was, "Suicide from causes unknown;" after this the coroner and the police retired, leaving the bereaved heir alone in the death-room, with the remains of that which had once been a living man.

★★★★★★

Scarcely a fortnight had elapsed from that day, ere the violin had been dusted, and four new, stout strings had been stretched upon it. Franz dared not look at them. He tried to play, but the bow trembled in his hand like a dagger in the grasp of a novice-brigand. He then determined not to try again, until the portentous night should arrive, when he should have a chance of rivalling, nay, of surpassing, Paganini.

The famous violinist had meanwhile left Paris, and was giving a series of triumphant concerts at an old Flemish town in Belgium.

5

One night, as Paganini, surrounded by a crowd of admirers, was sitting in the dining-room of the hotel at which he was staying, a visiting card, with a few words written on it in pencil, was handed to him by a young man with wild and staring eyes.

Fixing upon the intruder a look which few persons could bear, but receiving back a glance as calm and determined as his own, Paganini slightly bowed, and then dryly said:

"Sir, it shall be as you desire. Name the night. I am at your service."

On the following morning the whole town was startled by the appearance of bills posted at the corner of every street, and bearing the strange notice:

On the night of ..... at the Grand Theatre of ..... and for the first time, will appear before the public, Franz Stenio, a German violinist, arrived purposely to throw down the gauntlet to the world-famous Paganini and to challenge him to a duel—upon their violins. He purposes to compete with the great "*virtuoso*" in the execution of the most difficult of his compositions. The famous Paganini has accepted the challenge. Franz Stenio will play, in competition with the unrivalled violinist, the celebrated "Fantaisie Caprice" of the latter, known as "The Witches."

The effect of the notice was magical. Paganini, who, amid his greatest triumphs, never lost sight of a profitable speculation, doubled the usual price of admission, but still the theatre could not hold the crowds that flocked to secure tickets for that memorable performance.

★★★★★★

At last the morning of the concert day dawned, and the "duel" was in everyone's mouth. Franz Stenio, who, instead of sleeping, had passed the whole long hours of the preceding midnight in walking up and down his room like an encaged panther, had, toward morning, fallen on his bed from mere physical exhaustion. Gradually he passed into a death-like and dreamless slumber. At the gloomy winter dawn he awoke, but finding it too early to rise he fell to sleep again. And then he had a vivid dream—so vivid indeed, so life-like, that from its terrible realism he felt sure that it was a vision rather than a dream.

He had left his violin on a table by his bedside, locked in its case, the key of which never left him. Since he had strung it with those terrible chords he never let it out of his sight for a moment. In accordance with his resolution he had not touched it since his first trial, and his bow had never but once touched the human strings, for he had since always practised on another instrument. But now in his sleep he saw himself looking at the locked case. Something in it was attracting his attention, and he found himself incapable of detaching his eyes from it. Suddenly he saw the upper part of the case slowly rising, and, within the chink thus produced, he perceived two small, phosphorescent green eyes—eyes but too familiar to him—fixing themselves on his, lovingly, almost beseechingly. Then a thin, shrill voice, as if issuing from these ghastly orbs—the voice and orbs of Samuel Klaus himself—resounded in Stenio's horrified ear, and he heard it say:

"Franz, my beloved boy. . . . Franz, I cannot, no, *I cannot* separate myself from . . . . *them!*"

And "they" twanged piteously inside the case.

Franz stood speechless, horror-bound. He felt his blood actually freezing, and his hair moving and standing erect on his head. . . . .

"It's but a dream, an empty dream!" he attempted to formulate in his mind.

107

"I have tried my best, Franzchen..... I have tried my best to sever myself from these accursed strings, without pulling them to pieces ....." pleaded the same shrill, familiar voice. "Wilt thou help me to do so? ...."

Another twang, still more prolonged and dismal, resounded within the case, now dragged about the table in every direction, by some interior power, like some living wriggling thing, the twangs becoming sharper and more jerky with every new pull.

It was not for the first time that Stenio heard those sounds. He had often remarked them before—indeed, ever since he had used his master's *viscera* as a footstool for his own ambition. But on every occasion a feeling of creeping horror had prevented him from investigating their cause, and he had tried to assure himself that the sounds were only a hallucination.

But now he stood face to face with the terrible fact, whether in dream or in reality he knew not, nor did he care, since the hallucination—if hallucination it were—was far more real and vivid than any reality. He tried to speak, to take a step forward; but, as often happens in nightmares, he could neither utter a word nor move a finger..... He felt hopelessly paralyzed.

The pulls and jerks were becoming more desperate with each moment, and at last something inside the case snapped violently. The vision of his Stradivarius, devoid of its magical strings, flashed before his eyes, throwing him into a cold sweat of mute and unspeakable terror.

He made a superhuman effort to rid himself of the incubus that held him spell-bound. But as the last supplicating whisper of the invisible Presence repeated:

"Do, oh, do..... help me to cut myself off——"

Franz sprang to the case with one bound, like an enraged tiger defending its prey, and with one frantic effort breaking the spell.

"Leave the violin alone, you old fiend from hell!" he cried, in hoarse and trembling tones.

He violently shut down the self-raising lid, and while firmly pressing his left hand on it, he seized with the right a piece of rosin from the table and he drew on the leathered-covered top the sign of the six-pointed star—the seal used by King Solomon to bottle up the rebellious *djins* inside their prisons.

A wail, like the howl of a she-wolf moaning over her dead little ones, came out of the violin-case:

"Thou art ungrateful. . . . very ungrateful, my Franz!" sobbed the blubbering "spirit-voice." "But I forgive . . . . for I still love thee well. Yet thou canst not shut me in. . . . boy. Behold!"

And instantly a grayish mist spread over and covered case and table, and rising upward formed itself first into an indistinct shape. Then it began growing, and as it grew, Franz felt himself gradually enfolded in cold and damp coils, slimy as those of a huge snake. He gave a terrible cry and—awoke; but, strangely enough, not on his bed, but near the table, just as he had dreamed, pressing the violin-case desperately with both his hands.

"It was but a dream, . . . after all," he muttered, still terrified, but relieved of the load on his heaving breast.

With a tremendous effort he composed himself, and un-locked the case to inspect the violin. He found it covered with dust, but otherwise sound and in order, and he suddenly felt himself as cool and determined as ever. Having dusted the in-strument he carefully rosined the bow, tightened the strings and tuned them. He even went so far as to try upon it the first notes of the "Witches"; first cautiously and timidly, then using his bow boldly and with full force.

The sound of that loud, solitary note—defiant as the war trumpet of a conqueror, sweet and majestic as the touch of a seraph on his golden harp in the fancy of the faithful—thrilled through the very soul of Franz. It revealed to him a hitherto un-suspected potency in his bow, which ran on in strains that filled the room with the richest swell of melody, unheard by the art-ist until that night. Commencing in uninterrupted *legato* tones, his bow sang to him of sun-bright hope and beauty, of moonlit nights, when the soft and balmy stillness endowed every blade of grass and all things animate and inanimate with a voice and a song of love. For a few brief moments it was a torrent of melody,

"He violently shut down the self-raising lid and drew
on the leather-covered top the sign of the
six-pointed star, the seal of King Solomon."

the harmony of which, "tuned to soft woe," was calculated to make mountains weep, had there been any in the room, and to soothe—

even th' inexorable powers of hell,

. . . .the presence of which was undeniably felt in this modest hotel room. Suddenly, the solemn *legato* chant, contrary to all laws of harmony, quivered, became *arpeggios*, and ended in shrill *staccatos*, like the notes of a hyena laugh. The same creeping sensation of terror, as he had before felt, came over him, and Franz threw the bow away. He had recognised the familiar laugh, and would have no more of it. Dressing, he locked the bedevilled violin securely in its case, and, taking it with him to the dining-room, determined to await quietly the hour of trial.

6

The terrible hour of the struggle had come, and Stenio was at his post—calm, resolute, almost smiling.

The theatre was crowded to suffocation, and there was not even standing room to be got for any amount of hard cash or favouritism. The singular challenge had reached every quarter to which the post could carry it, and gold flowed freely into Paganini's unfathomable pockets, to an extent almost satisfying even to his insatiate and venal soul.

It was arranged that Paganini should begin. When he appeared upon the stage, the thick walls of the theatre shook to their foundations with the applause that greeted him. He began and ended his famous composition "The Witches" amid a storm of cheers. The shouts of public enthusiasm lasted so long that Franz began to think his turn would never come. When, at last, Paganini, amid the roaring applause of a frantic public, was allowed to retire behind the scenes, his eye fell upon Stenio, who was tuning his violin, and he felt amazed at the serene calmness, the air of assurance, of the unknown German artist.

When Franz approached the footlights, he was received with icy coldness. But for all that, he did not feel in the least disconcerted. He looked very pale, but his thin white lips wore a scornful smile as response to this dumb unwelcome. He was sure of his triumph.

At the first notes of the prelude of "The Witches" a thrill of astonishment passed over the audience. It was Paganini's touch, and—it was something more. Some—and they were the majority—thought that never, in his best moments of inspiration, had the Italian artist himself, in executing that diabolical composition of his, exhibited such an extraordinary diabolical power. Under the pressure of the long muscular fingers of Franz, the chords shivered like the palpitating intestines of a disembowelled victim under the vivisector's knife. They moaned melodiously, like a dying child. The large blue eye of the artist, fixed with a satanic expression upon the sounding-board, seemed to summon forth Orpheus himself from the infernal regions, rather than the musical notes supposed to be generated in the depths of the violin.

Sounds seemed to transform themselves into objective shapes, thickly and precipitately gathering as at the evocation of a mighty magician, and to be whirling around him, like a host of fantastic, infernal figures, dancing the witches' "goat dance." In the empty depths of the shadowy background of the stage, behind the artist, a nameless phantasmagoria, produced by the concussion of unearthly vibrations, seemed to form pictures of shameless orgies, of the voluptuous hymens of a real witches' Sabbat. . . . A collective hallucination took hold of the public. Panting for breath, ghastly, and trickling with the icy perspiration of an inexpressible horror, they sat spell-bound, and unable to break the spell of the music by the slightest motion. They experienced all the illicit enervating delights of the paradise of Mahommed, that come into the disordered fancy of an opium-eating Mussulman, and felt at the same time the abject terror, the agony of one who struggles against an attack of *delirium tremens*. . . . Many ladies shrieked aloud, others fainted, and strong men gnashed their teeth in a state of utter helplessness.

★★★★★★

Then came the *finale*. Thundering uninterrupted applause delayed its beginning, expanding the momentary pause to a duration of almost a quarter of an hour. The bravos were furious, almost hysterical. At last, when after a profound and last bow, Stenio, whose smile was as sardonic as it was triumphant, lifted his bow to attack the famous *finale*, his eye fell upon Paganini, who, calmly seated in the manager's box, had been behind none in zealous applause. The small and piercing black eyes of the Genoese artist were riveted to the Stradivarius in the hands of Franz, but otherwise he seemed quite cool and unconcerned. His rival's face troubled him for one short instant, but he regained his self-possession and, lifting once more his bow, drew the first note.

Then the public enthusiasm reached its acme, and soon knew no bounds. The listeners heard and saw indeed. The witches' voices resounded in the air, and beyond all the other voices, one voice was heard—

Discordant, and unlike to human sounds;

It seem'd of dogs the bark, of wolves the howl;
The doleful screechings of the midnight owl;
The hiss of snakes, the hungry lion's roar;
The sounds of billows beating on the shore;
The groan of winds among the leafy wood,
And burst of thunder from the rending cloud;—
'Twas these, all these in one. . . .

The magic bow was drawing forth its last quivering sounds— famous among prodigious musical feats—imitating the precipitate flight of the witches before bright dawn; of the unholy women saturated with the fumes of their nocturnal Saturnalia, when—a strange thing came to pass on the stage. Without the slightest transition, the notes suddenly changed. In their aerial flight of ascension and descent, their melody was unexpectedly altered in character. The sounds became confused, scattered, disconnected. . . . and then—it seemed from the sounding-board of the violin—came out squeaking, jarring tones, like those of a street Punch, screaming at the top of a senile voice:

"Art thou satisfied, Franz, my boy? . . . . Have not I gloriously kept my promise, eh?"

The spell was broken. Though still unable to realise the whole situation, those who heard the voice and the *Punchinello*-like tones, were freed, as by enchantment, from the terrible charm under which they had been held. Loud roars of laughter, mocking exclamations of half-anger and half-irritation were now heard from every corner of the vast theatre. The musicians in the orchestra, with faces still blanched from weird emotion, were now seen shaking with laughter, and the whole audience rose, like one man, from their seats, unable yet to solve the enigma; they felt, nevertheless, too disgusted, too disposed to laugh to remain one moment longer in the building.

But suddenly the sea of moving heads in the stalls and the pit became once more motionless, and stood petrified as though struck by lightning. What all saw was terrible enough—the handsome though wild face of the young artist suddenly aged, and his graceful, erect figure bent down, as though under the weight of years; but this was nothing to that which some of the most sensitive clearly perceived. Franz Stenio's person was now entirely enveloped in a semi-transparent mist, cloud-like, creeping with serpentine motion, and gradually tightening round the living form, as though ready to engulf him. And there were those also who discerned in this tall and ominous pillar of smoke a clearly-defined figure, a form showing the unmistakable outlines of a grotesque and grinning, but terribly awful-looking old man, whose *viscera* were protruding and the ends of the intestines stretched on the violin.

Within this hazy, quivering veil, the violinist was then seen, driving his bow furiously across the human chords, with the contortions of a demoniac, as we see them represented on medieval cathedral paintings!

An indescribable panic swept over the audience, and breaking now, for the last time, through the spell which had again bound them motionless, every living creature in the theatre made one mad rush towards the door. It was like the sudden outburst of a dam, a human torrent, roaring amid a shower of discordant notes, idiotic squeakings, prolonged and whining moans, cacophonous cries of frenzy, above which, like the detonations of pistol shots, was heard the consecutive bursting of the four strings stretched upon the sound-board of that bewitched violin.

★★★★★★

When the theatre was emptied of the last man of the audience, the terrified manager rushed on the stage in search of the unfortunate performer. He was found dead and already stiff, behind the footlights, twisted up into the most unnatural of postures, with the "catguts" wound curiously around his neck, and his violin shattered into a thousand fragments. . . .

When it became publicly known that the unfortunate would-be rival of Niccolo Paganini had not left a cent to pay for his funeral or his hotel bill, the Genoese, his proverbial meanness notwithstanding, settled the hotel-bill and had poor Stenio buried at his own expense.

He claimed, however, in exchange, the fragments of the Stradivarius—as a memento of the strange event.

An Unsolved Mystery

The circumstances attending the sudden death of M. Delessert, inspector of the *Police de Sûreté*, seems to have made such an impression upon the Parisian authorities that they were recorded in unusual detail. Omitting all particulars except what are necessary to explain matters, we reproduce here the undoubtedly strange history.

In the fall of 1861 there came to Paris a man who called himself Vic de Lassa, and was so inscribed upon his passport. He came from Vienna, and said he was a Hungarian, who owned estates on the borders of the Banat, not far from Zenta. He was a small man, aged thirty-five, with pale and mysterious face, long blonde hair, a vague, wandering blue eye, and a mouth of singular firmness. He dressed carelessly and ineffectively, and spoke and talked without much *empressement*. His companion, presumably his wife, on the other hand, ten years younger than himself, was a strikingly beautiful woman, of that dark, rich, velvety, luscious, pure Hungarian type which is so nigh akin to the gipsy blood. At the theatres, on the Bois, at the *cafés*, on the *boulevards*, and everywhere that idle Paris disports itself, Madame Aimée de Lassa attracted great attention and made a sensation.

They lodged in luxurious apartments on the Rue Richelieu, frequented the best places, received good company, entertained handsomely, and acted in every way as if possessed of considerable wealth. Lassa had always a good balance *chez* Schneider, Reuter et Cie., the Austrian Bankers in Rue de Rivoli, and wore diamonds of conspicuous lustre.

How did it happen then, that the Prefect of Police saw fit to suspect Monsieur and Madame de Lassa, and detailed Paul Delessert, one of the most *rusé* inspectors of the force, to "pipe" him? The fact is, the insignificant man with the splendid wife was a very mysterious personage, and it is the habit of the police to imagine that mystery always hides either the conspirator, the adventurer, or the charlatan. The conclusion to which the *prefect* had come in regard to M. de Lassa was that he was an adventurer and charlatan too. Certainly a successful one, then, for he was singularly unobtrusive and had in no way trumpeted the wonders which it was his mission to perform, yet in a few weeks after he had established himself in Paris the *salon* of M. de Lassa was the rage, and the number of persons who paid the fee of 100 *francs* for a single peep into his magic crystal, and a single message by his spiritual telegraph, was really astonishing. The secret of this was that M. de Lassa was a conjurer and diviner, whose pretensions were omniscient and whose predictions always came true.

Delessert did not find it very difficult to get an introduction and admission to de Lassa's *salon*. The receptions occurred every other day—two hours in the forenoon, three hours in the evening. It was evening when Inspector Delessert called in his assumed character of M. Flabry, *virtuoso* in jewels and a convert to Spiritualism. He found the handsome parlours brilliantly lighted, and a charming assemblage gathered of well-pleased guests, who did not at all seem to have come to learn their fortunes or fates, while contributing to the income of their host, but rather to be there out of complaisance to his virtues and gifts.

Mme. de Lassa performed upon the piano or conversed from group to group in a way that seemed to be delightful, while M. de Lassa walked about or sat in his insignificant, unconcerned way, saying a word now and then, but seeming to shun everything that was conspicuous. Servants handed about refreshments, ices, cordials, wines, etc., and Delessert could have fancied himself dropped in upon a quite modest evening entertainment, altogether *en règle*, but for one or two noticeable circumstances which his observant eyes quickly took in.

Except when their host or hostess was within hearing, the guests conversed together in low tones, rather mysteriously, and with not quite so much laughter as is usual on such occasions. At intervals a very tall and dignified footman would come to a guest, and, with a profound bow, present him a card on a silver salver. The guest would then go out, preceded by the solemn servant, but when he or she returned to the *salon*—some did not return at all—they invariably wore a dazed or puzzled look, were confused, astonished, frightened, or amused. All this was so unmistakably genuine, and de Lassa and his wife seemed so unconcerned amidst it all, not to say distinct from it all, that Delessert could not avoid being forcibly struck and considerably puzzled.

Two or three little incidents, which came under Delessert's own immediate observation, will suffice to make plain the character of the impressions made upon those present. A couple of gentlemen, both young, both of good social condition, and evidently very intimate friends, were conversing together and *tutoying* one another at a great rate, when the dignified footman summoned Alphonse. He laughed gaily. "Tarry a moment, *cher* Auguste," said he, "and thou shalt know all the particulars of this wonderful fortune!"

Eh bien!" responded Auguste, "may the oracle's mood be propitious!"

A minute had scarcely elapsed when Alphonse returned to the salon. His face was white and bore an appearance of concentrated rage that was frightful to witness. He came straight to Auguste, his eyes flashing, and bending his face toward his friend, who changed colour and recoiled, he hissed out, "Monsieur Lefébure, *vous êtes un lâche!*"

"Very well, Monsieur Meunier," responded Auguste, in the same low tone, "tomorrow morning at six o'clock!"

"It is settled, false friend, execrable traitor! *À la mort!*" rejoined Alphonse, walking off.

"*Cela va sans dire!*" muttered Auguste, going towards the hat-room.

A diplomatist of distinction, representative at Paris of a neighbouring state, an elderly gentleman of superb *aplomb* and most commanding appearance, was summoned to the oracle by the bowing footman. After being absent about five minutes he returned, and immediately made his way through the press to M. de Lassa, who was standing not far from the fireplace, with his hands in his pockets, and a look of utmost indifference upon his face. Delessert standing near, watched the interview with eager interest.

"I am exceedingly sorry," said General Von—, "to have to absent myself so soon from your interesting *salon*, M. de Lassa, but the result of my *séance* convinces me that my dispatches have been tampered with."

"I am sorry," responded M. de Lassa, with an air of languid but courteous interest, "I hope you may be able to discover which of your servants has been unfaithful."

"I am going to do that now," said the general, adding, in significant tones, "I shall see that both he and his accomplices do not escape severe punishment."

"That is the only course to pursue, *Monsieur le Comte.*" The ambassador stared, bowed, and took his leave with a bewilderment on his face that was beyond the power of his tact to control.

In the course of the evening M. de Lassa went carelessly to the piano, and, after some indifferent vague preluding, played a remarkably effective piece of music, in which the turbulent life and buoyancy of bacchanalian strains melted gently, almost imperceptibly away, into a sobbing wail of regret and languor, and weariness and despair. It was beautifully rendered, and made a great impression upon the guests, one of whom, a lady, cried, "How lovely, how sad! Did you compose that yourself, M. de Lassa?"

He looked towards her absently for an instant, then replied: "I? Oh, no! That is merely a reminiscence, *madame.*"

"Do you know who did compose it, M. de Lassa?" enquired

a *virtuoso* present.

"I believe it was originally written by Ptolemy Auletes, the father of Cleopatra," said M. de Lassa, in his indifferent, musing way, "but not in its present form. It has been twice rewritten to my knowledge; still, the air is substantially the same."

"From whom did you get it, M. de Lassa, if I may ask?" persisted the gentleman.

"Certainly! certainly! The last time I heard it played was by Sebastian Bach; but that was Palestrina's—the present—version. I think I prefer that of Guido of Arezzo—it is ruder, but has more force. I got the air from Guido himself."

"You—from—Guido!" cried the astonished gentleman,

"Yes, *monsieur*," answered de Lassa, rising from the piano with his usual indifferent air. "*Mon Dieu!*" cried the *virtuoso*, putting his hand to his head after the manner of Mr. Twemlow, "*Mon Dieu!* that was in *Anno Domini* 1022!"

"A little later than that—July 1031, if I remember rightly," courteously corrected M. de Lassa.

At this moment the tall footman bowed before M. Delessert, and presented the salver containing the card. Delessert took it and read:

"*On vous accorde trente-cinq secondes, M. Flabry, tout au plus!*"

Delessert followed the footman from the *salon* across the corridor. The footman opened the door of another room and bowed again, signifying that Delessert was to enter. "Ask no questions," he said briefly; "Sidi is mute." Delessert entered the room and the door closed behind him. It was a small room, with a strong smell of frankincense pervading it. The walls were covered completely with red hangings that concealed the windows, and the floor was felted with a thick carpet. Opposite the door, at the upper end of the room near the ceiling, was the face of a large clock; under it, each lighted by tall wax candles, were two small tables containing, the one an apparatus very like the common registering telegraph instrument, the other a crystal globe about twenty inches in diameter, set upon an exquisitely wrought tripod of gold and bronze intermingled. By the door stood Sidi, a man jet black in colour, wearing a white turban and *burnous*, and having a sort of wand of silver in one hand. With the other, he took Delessert by the right arm above the elbow, and led him quickly up the room. He pointed to the clock, and it struck an alarm; he pointed to the crystal.

Delessert bent over, looked into it and saw—a facsimile of his own sleeping-room, everything photographed exactly. Sidi did not give him time to exclaim, but still holding him by the arm, took him to the other table. The telegraph-like instrument began to *click-click*. Sidi opened the drawer, drew out a slip of paper, crammed it into Delessert's hand, and pointed to the clock, which struck again. The thirty-five seconds were expired. Sidi, still retaining hold of Delessert's arm, pointed to the door and led him towards it. The door opened, Sidi pushed him out, the door closed, the tall footman stood there bowing, the interview with the oracle was over. Delessert glanced at the piece of paper in his hand. It was a printed scrap, capital letters, and read simply:

To M. Paul Delessert: The policeman is always welcome; the spy is always in danger!

Delessert was dumbfounded a moment to find his disguise detected; but the words of the tall footman, "This way, if you please, M. Flabry," brought him to his senses. Setting his lips, he returned to the *salon*, and without delay sought M. de Lassa.

"Do you know the contents of this?" asked he, showing the message.

"I know everything, M. Delessert," answered de Lassa, in his careless way.

"Then perhaps you are aware that I mean to expose a charlatan, and unmask a hypocrite, or perish in the attempt?" said Delessert.

"*Cela m'est égal, monsieur,*" replied de Lassa.

"You accept my challenge, then?"

"Oh! it is a defiance, then?" replied de Lassa, letting his eye rest a moment upon Delessert, "*mais oui, je l'accepte!*" And thereupon Delessert departed.

Delessert now set to work, aided by all the forces the Prefect of Police could bring to bear, to detect and expose this consummate sorcerer, whom the ruder processes of our ancestors would easily have disposed of—by combustion. Persistent enquiry satisfied Delessert that the man was neither a Hungarian nor named de Lassa; that no matter how far back his power of "reminiscence" might extend, in his present and immediate form he had been born in this unregenerate world in the toy-making city of Nuremberg; that he was noted in boyhood for his great turn for ingenious manufactures, but was very wild, and a *mauvais sujet*. In his sixteenth year he had escaped to Geneva and apprenticed himself to a maker of watches and instruments.

Here he had been seen by the celebrated Robert Houdin, the *prestidigitateur*. Houdin, recognising the lad's talents, and being himself a maker of ingenious automata, had taken him off to Paris and employed him in his own workshops, as well as an assistant in the public performances of his amusing and curious *diablerie*. After staying with Houdin some years, Pflock Haslich (which was de Lassa's right name) had gone East in the suite of a Turkish *pasha*, and after many years' roving, in lands where he could not be traced under a cloud of pseudonyms, had finally turned up in Venice, and come thence to Paris.

Delessert next turned his attention to Mme. de Lassa. It was more difficult to get a clue by means of which to know her past life; but it was necessary in order to understand enough about Haslich. At last, through an accident, it became probable that Mme. Aimée was identical with a certain Mme. Schlaff, who had been rather conspicuous among the *demi-monde* of Buda. Delessert posted off to that ancient city, and thence went into the wilds of Transylvania to Medgyes. On his return, as soon as he reached the telegraph and civilization, he telegraphed the *prefect* from Karcag:

Don't lose sight of my man, nor let him leave Paris. I will run him in for you two days after I get back.

It happened that on the day of Delessert's return to Paris the *prefect* was absent, being with the emperor at Cherbourg. He came back on the fourth day, just twenty-four hours after the announcement of Delessert's death. That happened, as near as could be gathered, in this wise: the night after Delessert's return he was present at de Lassa's *salon* with a ticket of admittance to a *séance*. He was very completely disguised as a decrepit old man, and fancied that it was impossible for anyone to detect him. Nevertheless, when he was taken into the room, and looked into the crystal, he was actually horror-stricken to see there a picture of himself, lying face down and senseless upon the side-walk of a street; and the message he received read thus:

What you have seen will be Delessert, in three days. Prepare!

The detective, unspeakably shocked, retired from the house at once, and sought his own lodgings.

In the morning he came to the office in a state of extreme dejection. He was completely unnerved. In relating to a brother inspector what had occurred, he said: "That man can do what he promises, I am doomed!"

He said that he thought he could make a complete case out against Haslich *alias* de Lassa, but could not do so without seeing the *prefect*, and getting instructions. He would tell nothing in regard to his discoveries in Buda and in Transylvania—said that he was not at liberty to do so—and repeatedly exclaimed: "Oh! if *M. le Préfet* were only here!" He was told to go to the *prefect* at Cherbourg, but refused, upon the ground that his presence was needed in Paris. He time and again averred his conviction that he was a doomed man, and showed himself both vacillating and irresolute in his conduct, and extremely nervous. He was told that he was perfectly safe, since de Lassa and all his household were under constant surveillance; to which he replied; "You do not know the man."

An inspector was detailed to accompany Delessert, never lose sight of him night and day, and guard him carefully; and proper precautions were taken in regard to his food and drink, while the guards watching de Lassa were doubled.

On the morning of the third day, Delessert, who had been staying chiefly indoors, avowed his determination to go at once and telegraph to *M. le Préfet* to return immediately. With this intention he and his brother-officer started out. Just as they got to the corner of the Rue de Lancry and the Boulevard, Delessert stopped suddenly and put his hand to his forehead.

"My God!" he cried, "the crystal! the picture!" and he fell prone upon his face, insensible. He was taken at once to a hospital, but only lingered a few hours, never regaining his consciousness. Under express instructions from the authorities, a most careful, minute, and thorough autopsy was made of Delessert's body by several distinguished surgeons, whose unanimous opinion was, that the cause of his death was apoplexy, due to fatigue and nervous excitement.

As soon as Delessert was sent to the hospital, his brother-inspector hurried to the Central Office, and de Lassa, together with his wife and every one connected with the establishment, were at once arrested. De Lassa smiled contemptuously as they took him away. "I knew you were coming; I prepared for it. You will be glad to release me again."

It was quite true that de Lassa had prepared for them.

When the house was searched, it was found that every paper had been burned, the crystal globe was destroyed, and in the room of the *séances* was a great heap of delicate machinery broken into indistinguishable bits. "That cost me 200,000 *francs*," said de Lassa, pointing to the pile, "but it has been a good investment."

The walls and floors were ripped out in several places, and the damage to the property was considerable. In prison neither de Lassa nor his associates made any revelations. The notion that they had something to do with Delessert's death was quickly dispelled, in a legal point of view, and all the party but de Lassa were released. He was still detained in prison, upon one pretext or another, when one morning he was found hanging by a silk sash to the cornice of the room where he was confined—dead.

The night before, it was afterwards discovered, "*Madame*" de Lassa had eloped with a tall footman, taking the Nubian Sidi with them.

De Lassa's secrets died with him.

A Story of the Mystical
A.k.a. *Can the 'Double' Murder?*

To the Editor of *The Sun*.

Sir, — One morning in 1867 Eastern Europe was startled by news of the most horrifying description. Michael Obrenovitch, reigning Prince of Serbia, his aunt, the Princess Catherine, or Katinka, and her daughter had been murdered in broad daylight, near Belgrade, in their own garden, assassin or assassins remaining unknown. The prince had received several bullet-shots and stabs, and his body was actually butchered; the princess was killed on the spot, her head smashed, and her young daughter, though still alive, was not expected to survive.

The circumstances are too recent to have been forgotten, but in that part of the world, at the time, the case created a delirium of excitement.

In the Austrian dominions and in those under the doubtful protectorate of Turkey, from Bucharest down to Trieste, no high family felt secure. In those half-Oriental countries every Montecchi has its Capuletti, and it was rumoured that the bloody deed was perpetrated by the Prince Kara-Gueorguevitch, or "Tzerno-Gueorgey," as he is usually called in those parts. Several persons innocent of the act were, as is usual in such cases, imprisoned, and the real murderers escaped justice. A young relative of the victim, greatly beloved by his people, a mere child, taken for the purpose from a school in Paris, was brought over in ceremony to Belgrade and proclaimed Hospodar of Serbia. In the turmoil of political excitement the tragedy of Belgrade was forgotten by all but an old Serbian matron who had been attached to the Obrenovitch family, and who, like Rachel, would not be comforted for the death of her children. After the proclamation of the young Obrenovitch, nephew of the murdered man, she had sold out her property and disappeared; but not before taking a solemn vow on the tombs of the victims to avenge their deaths.

The writer of this truthful narrative had passed a few days at Belgrade, about three months before the horrid deed was perpetrated, and knew the Princess Katinka. She was a kind, gentle and lazy creature at home; abroad she seemed a Parisian in manners and education. As nearly all the personages who will figure in this true story are still living, it is but decent that I should withhold their names, and give only initials.

The old Serbian lady seldom left her house, going out but to see the princess occasionally. Crouched on a pile of pillows and carpeting, clad in the picturesque national dress, she looked like the Cumaean Sibyl in her days of calm repose. Strange stories were whispered about her occult knowledge, and thrilling accounts circulated sometimes among the guests assembled round the fireside of my modest inn. Our fat landlord's maiden aunt's cousin had been troubled for some time past by a wandering vampire, and had been bled nearly to death by the nocturnal visitor; and while the efforts and exorcisms of the parish pope had been of no avail, the victim was luckily delivered by Gospoja P——, who had put to flight the disturbing ghost by merely shaking her fist at him, and shaming him in his own language.

It was in Belgrade that I learned for the first time this highly interesting fact for philology, namely, that spooks have a language of their own. The old lady, whom I will call Gospoja P——, was generally attended by another personage destined to be the principal actress in our tale of horror. It was a young gypsy girl, from some part of Rumania, about fourteen years of age. Where she was born, and who she was, she seemed to know as little as anyone else. I was told she had been brought one day by a party of strolling gypsies, and left in the yard of the old lady; from which moment she became an inmate of the house. She was nicknamed "the sleeping girl," as she was said to be gifted with the faculty of apparently dropping asleep wherever she stood, and speaking her dreams aloud. The girl's heathen name was Frosya.

About eighteen months after the news of the murder had reached Italy, where I was at the time, I was travelling over the Banat, in a small wagon of my own, hiring a horse whenever I needed it, after the fashion of this primitive, trusting country. I met on my way an old Frenchman, a scientist, travelling alone after my own fashion, but with the difference that while he was a pedestrian I dominated the road from the eminence of a throne of dry hay, in a jolting wagon. I discovered him one fine morning, slumbering in a wilderness of shrubs and flowers, and had nearly passed over him, absorbed as I was, in the contemplation of the surrounding glorious scenery. The acquaintance was soon made, no great ceremony of mutual introduction being needed. I had heard his name mentioned in circles interested in mesmerism, and knew him to be a powerful adept of the school of Du Potet.

"I have found," he remarked in the course of the conversation, after I had made him share my seat of hay, "one of the most wonderful subjects in this lovely *Thebaide*. I have an appointment tonight with the family. They are seeking to unravel the mystery of a murder by means of the clairvoyance of the girl. . . . . . . She is wonderful; very, very wonderful!"

"Who is she?" I asked.

"A Rumanian gypsy. She was brought up, it appears, in the family of the Serbian reigning prince, who reigns no more, for he was very mysteriously mur——. *Halloo*, take care! *Diable*, you will upset us over the precipice!" he hurriedly exclaimed, unceremoniously snatching from me the reins, and giving the horse a violent pull.

"You do not mean Prince Obrenovitch?" I asked, aghast.

"Yes, I do; and him precisely. Tonight I have to be there, hoping to close a series of *séances* by finally developing a most marvellous manifestation of the hidden power of human spirit, and you may come with me. I will introduce you; and, besides, you can help me as an interpreter, for they do not speak French."

As I was pretty sure that if the somnambule was Frosya, the rest of the family must be Gospoja P——, I readily accepted. At sunset we were at the foot of the mountain, leading to the old castle, as the Frenchman called the place. It fully deserved the poetical name given it. There was a rough bench in the depths of one of the shadowy retreats, and as we stopped at the entrance of this poetical place, and the Frenchman was gallantly busying himself with my horse on the suspicious-looking bridge which led across the water to the entrance gate, I saw a tall figure slowly rise from the bench and come toward us. It was my old friend, Gospoja P——, looking more pale and more mysterious than ever. She exhibited no surprise at seeing me, but simply greeting me after the Serbian fashion, with a triple kiss on both cheeks, she took hold of my hand and led me straight to the nest of ivy. Half reclining on a small carpet spread on the tall grass with her back leaning against the wall, I recognised our Frosya.

She was dressed in the national costume of the Wallachian women, a sort of gauze turban intermingled with various gilt medals and bands on her head, white shirt with opened sleeves, and petticoats of variegated colours. Her face looked deadly pale, her eyes were closed, and her countenance presented that stony, sphinx-like look which characterizes in such a peculiar way the entranced clairvoyant somnambule. If it were not for the heaving motion of her chest and bosom, ornamented by rows of medals and bead necklaces which feebly tinkled at every breath, one might have thought her dead, so lifeless and corpse-like was her face. The Frenchman informed me that he had sent her to sleep just as we were approaching the house, and that she now was as he had left her the previous night: he then began busying himself with the *sujet*, as he called Frosya.

Paying no further attention to us, he shook her by the hand, and then making a few rapid passes, stretched out her arm and stiffened it. The arm, as rigid as iron, remained in that position.

He then closed all her fingers but one—the middle finger—which he caused to point at the evening star, which twinkled in the deep blue sky. Then he turned round and went over from right to left, throwing on some of his fluids here, again discharging them at another place; busying himself with his invisible but potent fluids, like a painter with his brush when giving the last touches to a picture.

The old lady, who had silently watched him, with her chin in her hand the while, put out her thin, skeleton-looking hand on his arm and arrested it, as he was preparing himself to begin the regular mesmeric passes.

"Wait," she whispered, "till the star is set, and the ninth hour completed. The *vourdalaki* (Russian vampires) are hovering around; they may spoil the influence."

"What does she say?" inquired the mesmeriser, annoyed at her interference.

I explained to him that the old lady feared the pernicious influences of the *vourdalaki*.

"*Vourdalaki?* What's that, the *vourdalaki?*" exclaimed the Frenchman. "Let us be satisfied with Christian spirits, if they honour us tonight with a visit, and lose no time for the *vourdalaki*."

I glanced at the Gospoja. She had become deathly pale, and her brow was sternly knitted over her flashing black eyes.

"Tell him not to jest at this hour of the night!" she cried. "He does not know the country. Even the Holy Church may fail to protect us, once the *vourdalaki* aroused. What's this?" pushing with her foot a bundle of herbs the botanizing mesmeriser had laid near on the grass. She bent over the collection and anxiously examined the contents of the bundle, after which she flung the whole in the water.

"It must not be left here," she firmly added; "these are the St. John's plants, and they might attract the wandering ones."

Meanwhile the night had come, and the moon illuminated the landscape with a pale, ghostly light. The nights in the Banat are nearly as beautiful as in the East, and the Frenchman had to go on with his experiments in the open air as the "pope" of the Church had prohibited such in his tower, which was used as the parsonage, for fear of filling the holy precincts with the heretical devils of the mesmeriser, which, he remarked, he would be unable to exorcise on account of their being foreigners.

The old gentleman had thrown off his travelling blouse, rolled up his shirt sleeves, and now striking a theatrical attitude began a regular process of mesmerisation. Under his quivering fingers the odile fluid actually seemed to flash in the twilight. Frosya was placed with her figure facing the moon, and every motion of the entranced girl was discernible as in daylight. In a few minutes large drops of perspiration appeared on her brow and slowly rolled down her pale face, glittering in the moonbeams. Then she moved uneasily about and began chanting a low melody, to the words of which the Gospoja, anxiously bent over the unconscious girl, was listening with avidity and trying to catch every syllable. With her thin finger on her lips her eyes nearly starting from their sockets, her frame motionless, the old lady seemed herself transfixed into a statue of attention.

The group was a remarkable one, and I regretted that I was not a painter. What followed was a scene worthy to figure in *Macbeth*. At one side the slender girl, pale and corpse-like, writhing under the invisible fluid of him who for the hour was her omnipotent master; at the other the old matron, who, burning with her unquenched desire of revenge, stood like the picture of Nemesis, waiting for the long-expected name of the prince's murderer to be at last pronounced. The Frenchman himself seemed transfigured, his gray hair standing on end; his bulky, clumsy form seemed to have grown in a few minutes. All theatrical pretence was now gone; there remained but the mesmeriser, aware of his responsibility, unconscious himself of the possible results, studying and anxiously expecting.

Suddenly Frosya, as if lifted by some supernatural force, rose from her reclining posture and stood erect before us, motionless and still again, waiting for the magnetic fluid to direct her. The Frenchman, silently taking the old lady's hand, placed it in that of the somnambulist, and ordered her to put herself *en rapport* with the Gospoja.

"What seest thou, my daughter?" softly murmured the Serbian lady. "Can your spirit seek out the murderers?"

"Search and behold!" sternly commanded the mesmeriser, fixing his gaze upon the face of the subject.

"I am—on my way—I go," faintly whispered Frosya, her voice seeming not to come from herself, but from the surrounding atmosphere.

At this moment something so extraordinary took place that I doubt my ability to describe it. A luminous shadow, vapour-like, appeared closely surrounding the girl's body. At first about an inch in thickness, it gradually expanded, and, gathering itself, suddenly seemed to break off from the body altogether, and condense itself into a kind of semi-solid vapour, which very soon assumed the likeness of the somnambule herself. Flickering about the surface of the earth, the form vacillated for two or three seconds, then glided noiselessly toward the river. It disappeared like a mist dissolved in the moonbeams, which seemed to absorb and imbibe it altogether.

I had followed the scene with intense attention The mysterious operation, known in the East as the evocation of the *scîn-lâc* was taking place before my own eyes To doubt was impossible, and Du Potet was right in saying that mesmerism is the conscious magic of the ancients, and spiritualism the unconscious effect of the same magic upon certain organisms.

As soon as the vaporous double had soaked itself through the pores of the girl, the Gospoja had, by a rapid motion of the hand which was left free, drawn from under her *pelisse* something which looked to us suspiciously like a small stiletto, and placed it as rapidly in the girl's bosom. The action was so quick that the mesmeriser, absorbed in his work, had not remarked it, as he afterwards told me. A few minutes elapsed in a dead silence. We seemed a group of petrified persons. Suddenly a thrilling and transpiercing cry burst from the entranced girl's lips. She bent forward, and snatching the stiletto from her bosom, plunged it furiously around her in the air, as if pursuing imaginary foes. Her mouth foamed, and incoherent, wild exclamations broke from her lips, among which discordant sounds I discerned several times two familiar Christian names of men. The mesmeriser was so terrified that he lost all control over himself, and instead of withdrawing the fluid, he loaded the girl with it still more.

"Take care!" exclaimed I. "Stop! You will kill her or she will kill you!"

But the Frenchman had unwittingly raised subtle potencies of nature, over which he had no control. Furiously turning round, the girl struck at him a blow which would have killed him, had he not avoided it by jumping aside, receiving but a severe scratch on the right arm. The poor man was panic-stricken. Climbing with an extraordinary agility for a man of his bulky form on the wall over her, he fixed himself on it astride, and gathering the remnants of his will power, sent in her direction a series of passes. At the second, the girl dropped the weapon and remained motionless.

"What are you about?" hoarsely shouted the mesmeriser in French, seated like some monstrous night goblin on the wall. . "Answer me: I command you!"

"I did—but what she—whom you ordered me to obey—commanded me do," answered the girl in French, to my amazement.

"What did the old witch command you?" irreverently asked he.

"To find them—who murdered—kill them—I did so—and they are no more!—avenged—avenged! They are—"

An exclamation of triumph, a loud shout of infernal joy rang loud in the air, and awakening the dogs of the neighbouring villages a responsive howl of barking began from that moment like a ceaseless echo of the Gospoja's cry.

"I am avenged. I feel it, I know it. My warning heart tells me that the fiends are no more." And she fell panting on the ground, dragging down in her fall the girl, who allowed herself to be pulled down as if she were a bag of wool.

"I hope my subject did no further mischief tonight. She is a dangerous as well as a very wonderful subject!" said the Frenchman.

We parted. Three days after that I was at T——, and as I was sitting in the dining-room of a restaurant waiting for my lunch I happened to pick up a newspaper, and the first lines I read ran thus:

Vienna, 186——. Two Mysterious Deaths.

Last evening, at 9:45, as P—— was about to retire, two of the gentlemen in waiting suddenly exhibited great terror, as though they had seen a dreadful apparition. They screamed, staggered, and ran about the room holding up their hands as if to ward off the blows of an unseen weapon. They paid no attention to the eager questions of the prince and suite, but presently fell writhing upon the floor, and expired in great agony.

Their bodies exhibited no appearance of apoplexy, nor any external marks of wounds; but wonderful to relate, there were numerous dark spots and long marks upon the skin, as though they were stabs and slashes made without puncturing the cuticle. The autopsy revealed the fact that beneath each of these mysterious discolorations there was a deposit of coagulated blood. The greatest excitement prevails, and the faculty are unable to solve the mystery.

A Witch's Den

Our kind host Sham Rao was very gay during the remaining hours of our visit. He did his best to entertain us, and would not hear of our leaving the neighbourhood without having seen its greatest celebrity, its most interesting sight. A *jadu wâlâ*—sorceress—well known in the district, was just at this time under the influence of seven sister-goddesses, who took possession of her by turns, and spoke their oracles through her lips. Sham Rao said we must not fail to see her, be it only in the interests of science.

The evening closes in, and we once more get ready for an excursion. It is only five miles to the cavern of the Pythia of Hindostan; the road runs through a jungle, but it is level and smooth. Besides, the jungle and its ferocious inhabitants have ceased to frighten us. The timid elephants we had in the "dead city" are sent home, and we are to mount new behemoths belonging to a neighbouring *râjâ*. The pair that stand before the verandah like two dark hillocks are steady and trustworthy. Many a time these two have hunted the royal tiger, and no wild shrieking or thunderous roaring can frighten them. And so, let us start!

The ruddy flames of the torches dazzle our eyes and increase the forest gloom. Our surroundings seem so dark, so mysterious. There is something indescribably fascinating, almost solemn, in these night-journeys in the out-of-the-way corners of India. Everything is silent and deserted around you, everything is dozing on the earth and overhead. Only the heavy, regular tread of the elephants breaks the stillness of the night, like the sound of falling hammers in the underground smithy of Vulcan. From time to time uncanny voices and murmurs are heard in the black forest.

"The wind sings its strange song amongst the ruins," says one of us, "what a wonderful acoustic phenomenon!"

"*Bhûta, bhûta!*" whisper the awestruck torch-bearers. They brandish their torches and swiftly spin on one leg, and snap their fingers to chase away the aggressive spirits.

The plaintive murmur is lost in the distance. The forest is once more filled with the cadences of its invisible nocturnal life—the metallic whirr of the crickets, the feeble, monotonous croak of the tree-frog, the rustle of the leaves. From time to time all this suddenly stops short and then begins again, gradually increasing and increasing.

Heavens! What teeming life, what stores of vital energy are hidden under the smallest leaf, the most imperceptible blades of grass, in this tropical forest! Myriads of stars shine in the dark blue of the sky, and myriads of fireflies twinkle at us from every bush, moving sparks, like a pale reflection of the far-away stars.

We left the thick forest behind us, and reached a deep glen, on three sides bordered with the thick forest, where even by day the shadows are as dark as by night. We were about two thousand feet above the foot of the Vindhya ridge, judging by the ruined wall of Mandu, straight above our heads.

Suddenly a very chilly wind rose that nearly blew our torches out. Caught in the labyrinth of bushes and rocks, the wind angrily shook the branches of the blossoming syringas, then, shaking itself free, it turned back along the glen and flew down the valley, howling, whistling and shrieking, as if all the fiends of the forest together were joining in a funeral song.

"Here we are," said Sham Rao, dismounting. "Here is the village; the elephants cannot go any further."

"The village? Surely you are mistaken. I don't see anything but trees."

"It is too dark to see the village. Besides, the huts are so small, and so hidden by the bushes, that even by daytime you could hardly find them. And there is no light in the houses, for fear of the spirits."

"And where is your witch? Do you mean we are to watch

her performance in complete darkness?"

Sham Rao cast a furtive, timid look round him; and his voice, when he answered our questions, was somewhat tremulous.

"I implore you not to call her a witch! She may hear you.... It is not far off, it is not more than half a mile. Do not allow this short distance to shake your decision. No elephant, and not even a horse, could make its way there. We must walk.... But we shall find plenty of light there...."

This was unexpected, and far from agreeable. To walk in this gloomy Indian night; to scramble through thickets of cactuses; to venture in a dark forest, full of wild animals—this was too much for Miss X—. She declared that she would go no further. She would wait for us in the *howdah* on the elephant's back, and perhaps would go to sleep.

Narayan was against this *parti de plaisir* from the very beginning, and now, without explaining his reasons, he said she was the only sensible one among us.

"You won't lose anything," he remarked, "by staying where you are. And I only wish everyone would follow your example."

"What ground have you for saying so, I wonder?" remonstrated Sham Rao, and a slight note of disappointment rang in his voice, when he saw that the excursion, proposed and organized by himself, threatened to come to nothing. "What harm could be done by it? I won't insist any more that the 'incarnation of gods' is a rare sight, and that the Europeans hardly ever have an opportunity of witnessing it; but, besides, the Kangalim in question is no ordinary woman. She leads a holy life; she is a prophetess, and her blessing could not prove harmful to anyone. I insisted on this excursion out of pure patriotism."

"*Sahib*, if your patriotism consists in displaying before foreigners the worst of our plagues, then why did you not order all the lepers of your district to assemble and parade before the eyes of our guests? You are a *patèl*, you have the power to do it."

How bitterly Narayan's voice sounded to our unaccustomed ears. Usually he was so even-tempered, so indifferent to everything belonging to the exterior world.

Fearing a quarrel between the Hindus, the colonel remarked,

in a conciliatory tone, that it was too late for us to reconsider our expedition. Besides, without being a believer in the "incarnation of gods," he was personally firmly convinced that demoniacs existed even in the West. He was eager to study every psychological phenomenon, wherever he met with it, and whatever shape it might assume.

It would have been a striking sight for our European and American friends if they had beheld our procession on that dark night. Our way lay along a narrow winding path up the mountain. Not more than two people could walk together—and we were thirty, including the torch-bearers. Surely some reminiscence of night sallies against the Confederate Southerners had revived in the colonel's breast, judging by the readiness with which he took upon himself the leadership of our small expedition. He ordered all the rifles and revolvers to be loaded, despatched three torch-bearers to march ahead of us, and arranged us in pairs. Under such a skilled chieftain we had nothing to fear from tigers; and so our procession started, and slowly crawled up the winding path.

It cannot be said that the inquisitive travellers, who appeared later on, in the den of the prophetess of Mandu, shone through the freshness and elegance of their costumes. My gown, as well as the travelling suits of the colonel and of Mr. Y— were nearly torn to pieces. The cactuses gathered from us whatever tribute they could, and the *Babu's* dishevelled hair swarmed with a whole colony of grasshoppers and fireflies, which probably, were attracted thither by the smell of cocoanut oil. The stout Sham Rao panted like a steam engine. Narayan alone was like his usual self—that is to say, like a bronze Hercules, armed with a club. At the last abrupt turn of the path, after having surmounted the difficulty of climbing over huge, scattered stones, we suddenly found ourselves on a perfectly smooth place; our eyes, in spite of our many torches, were dazzled with light, and our ears were struck by a medley of unusual sounds.

A new glen opened before us, the entrance of which, from the valley, was well masked by thick trees. We understood how easily we might have wandered round it, without ever suspecting its existence. At the bottom of the glen we discovered the abode of the celebrated Kangalim.

The den, as it turned out, was situated in the ruin of an old Hindu temple in tolerably good preservation. In all probability it was built long before the "Dead City," because during the epoch of the latter, the heathen were not allowed to have their own places of worship; and the temple stood quite close to the wall of the town, in fact, right under it. The cupolas of the two smaller lateral pagodas had fallen long ago, and huge bushes grew out of their altars. This evening their branches were hidden under a mass of bright-coloured rags, bits of ribbon, little pots, and various other talismans, because, even in them, popular superstition sees something sacred.

"And are not these poor people right? Did not these bushes grow on sacred ground? Is not their sap impregnated with the incense of offerings, and the exhalations of holy anchorites, who once lived and breathed here?"

The learned but superstitious Sham Rao would only answer our questions by new questions.

But the central temple, built of red granite, stood unharmed by time, and, as we learned afterwards, a deep tunnel opened just behind its closely-shut door. What was beyond it no one knew. Sham Rao assured us that no man of the last three generations had ever stepped over the threshold of this thick iron door; no one had seen the subterranean passage for many years. Kangalim lived there in perfect isolation, and, according to the oldest people in the neighbourhood, she had always lived there. Some people said she was three hundred years old; others alleged that a certain old man on his death-bed had revealed to his son that this old woman was no one else than *his own uncle*. This fabulous uncle had settled in the cave in the times when the "Dead City" still counted several hundreds of inhabitants. The hermit, busy paving his road to Moksha, had no intercourse with the rest of the world, and nobody knew how he lived and what he ate. But a good while ago, in the days when the *bellati* (foreigners) had not yet taken possession of this mountain, the old hermit suddenly was transformed into a hermitess. She continues his pursuits and speaks with his voice, and often in his name; but she receives worshippers, which was not the practice of her predecessor.

We had come too early, and the Pythia did not at first appear. But the square before the temple was full of people, and a wild though picturesque scene it was. An enormous bonfire blazed in the centre, and round it crowded the naked savages like so many black gnomes, adding whole branches of trees sacred to the seven sister-goddesses. Slowly and evenly they all jumped from one leg to another to a tune of a single monotonous musical phrase, which they repeated in chorus, accompanied by several local drums and tambourines. The hushed trill of the latter mingled with the forest echoes and the hysterical moans of two little girls, who lay under a heap of leaves by the fire. The poor children were brought here by their mothers, in the hope that the goddesses would take pity upon them and banish the two evil spirits under whose obsession they were. Both mothers were quite young, and sat on their heels blankly and sadly staring at the flames. No one paid us the slightest attention when we appeared, and afterwards during all our stay these people acted as if we were invisible. Had we worn a cap of darkness they could not have behaved more strangely.

"They feel the approach of the gods! The atmosphere is full of their sacred emanations!" mysteriously explained Sham Rao, contemplating with reverence the natives, whom his beloved Haeckel might have easily mistaken for his "missing link," the brood of his *Bathybius Haeckelii*.

"They are simply under the influence of toddy and opium!" retorted the irreverent *babu*.

The lookers-on moved as in a dream, as if they all were only half-awakened somnambulists, but the actors were simply victims of St. Vitus's dance. One of them, a tall old man, a mere skeleton with a long white beard, left the ring and begun whirling vertiginously, with his arms spread like wings, and loudly grinding his long, wolf-like teeth. He was painful and disgusting to look at. He soon fell down, and was carelessly, almost mechanically pushed aside by the feet of the others still engaged in their demoniac performance.

All this was frightful enough, but many more horrors were in store for us.

Waiting for the appearance of the *prima donna* of this forest opera company, we sat down on the trunk of a fallen tree, ready to ask innumerable questions of our condescending host. But I was hardly seated when a feeling of indescribable astonishment and horror made me shrink back.

I beheld the skull of a monstrous animal, the like of which I could not find in my zoological reminiscences.

This head was much larger than the head of an elephant skeleton. And still it could not be anything but an elephant, judging by the skilfully restored trunk, which wound down to my feet like a gigantic black leech. But an elephant has no horns, whereas this one had four of them! The front pair stuck from the flat forehead slightly bending forward and then spreading out; and the others had a wide base, like the root of a deer's horn, that gradually decreased almost up to the middle, and bore long branches enough to decorate a dozen ordinary elks. Pieces of the transparent amber-yellow rhinoceros skin were strained over the empty eye-holes of the skull, and small lamps burning behind them only added to the horror, the devilish appearance of this head.

"What can this be?" was our unanimous question. None of us had ever met anything like it, and even the colonel looked aghast.

"It is a Sivatherium," said Narayan. "Is it possible you never came across these fossils in European museums? Their remains are common enough in the Himalayas, though, of course, in fragments. They were called after Shiva."

"If the collector of this district ever hears that this antediluvian relic adorns the den of your—ahem!—witch," remarked the *babu*, "it won't adorn it many days longer."

All around the skull and on the floor of the portico there were heaps of white flowers, which, though not quite antediluvian, were totally unknown to us. They were as large as a big rose, and their white petals were covered with a red powder, the inevitable concomitant of every Indian religious ceremony. Further on there were groups of cocoanuts, and large brass dishes filled with rice, each adorned with a red or green taper. In the centre of the portico there stood a queer-shaped censer, surrounded with chandeliers. A little boy, dressed from head to foot in white, threw into it handfuls of aromatic powders.

"These people, who assemble here to worship Kangalim," said Sham Rao, "do not actually belong either to her sect or to any other. They are devil-worshippers. They do not believe in Hindu gods; they live in small communities; they belong to one of the many Indian races which usually are called the hill-tribes. Unlike the Shanars of Southern Travancore, they do not use the blood of sacrificial animals; they do not build separate temples to their *bhutas*. But they are possessed by the strange fancy that the goddess Kâli, the wife of Shiva, from time immemorial has had a grudge against them, and sends her favourite evil spirits to torture them. Save this little difference, they have the same beliefs as the Shanars. God does not exist for them; and even Shiva is considered by them as an ordinary spirit. Their chief worship is offered to the souls of the dead.

"These souls, however righteous and kind they may be in their lifetime, become after death as wicked as can be; they are happy only when they are torturing living men and cattle. As the opportunities of doing so are the only reward for the virtues they possessed when incarnated, a very wicked man is punished by becoming after his death a very soft-hearted ghost; he loathes his loss of daring, and is altogether miserable. The results of this strange logic are not bad, nevertheless. These savages and devil-worshippers are the kindest and the most truth-loving of all the hill-tribes. They do whatever they can to be worthy of their ultimate reward; because, don't you see, they all long to become the wickedest of devils!"

And put in good humour by his own wittiness, Sham Rao laughed till his hilarity became offensive, considering the sacredness of the place.

"A year ago some business matters sent me to Tinevelli," continued he. "Staying with a friend of mine, who is a Shanar, I was allowed to be present at one of the ceremonies in the honour of devils. No European has as yet witnessed this worship, whatever the missionaries may say; but there are many converts amongst the Shanars, who willingly describe them to the *padres*. My friend is a wealthy man, which is probably the reason why the devils are especially vicious to him. They poison his cattle, spoil his crops and his coffee plants, and persecute his numerous relations, sending them sunstrokes, madness and epilepsy, over which illnesses they especially preside. These wicked demons have settled in every corner of his spacious landed property—in the woods, the ruins, and even in his stables.

"To avert all this, my friend covered his land with *stucco* pyramids, and prayed humbly, asking the demons to draw their portraits on each of them, so that he may recognize them and worship each of them separately, as the rightful owner of this, or that, particular pyramid. And what do you think?... Next morning all the pyramids were found covered with drawings. Each of them bore an incredibly good likeness of the dead of the neighbourhood. My friend had known personally almost all of them. He found also a portrait of his own late father amongst the lot."

"Well? And was he satisfied?"

"Oh, he was very glad, very satisfied. It enabled him to choose the right thing to gratify the personal tastes of each demon, don't you see? He was not vexed at finding his father's portrait. His father was somewhat irascible; once he nearly broke both his son's legs, administering to him fatherly punishment with an iron bar, so that he could not possibly be very dangerous after his death. But another portrait, found on the best and the prettiest of the pyramids, amazed my friend a good deal, and put him in a blue funk. The whole district recognised an English officer, a certain Captain Pole, who in his lifetime was as kind a gentleman as ever lived."

"Indeed? But do you mean to say that this strange people worshipped Captain Pole also?"

"Of course they did! Captain Pole was such a worthy man, such an honest officer, that, after his death, he could not help being promoted to the highest rank of Shanar devils. The Pe-

Kovil, demon's-house, sacred to his memory, stands side by side with the Pe-Kovil Bhadrakâlî, which was recently conferred on the wife of a certain German missionary, who also was a most charitable lady and so is very dangerous now."

"But what are their ceremonies? Tell us something about their rites."

"Their rites consist chiefly of dancing, singing, and killing sacrificial animals. The Shanars have no castes, and eat all kinds of meat. The crowd assembles about the Pe-Kovil, previously designated by the priest; there is a general beating of drums, and slaughtering of fowls, sheep and goats. When Captain Pole's turn came an ox was killed, as a thoughtful attention to the peculiar tastes of his nation. The priest appeared, covered with bangles, and holding a wand on which tinkled numberless little bells, and wearing garlands of red and white flowers round his neck, and a black mantle, on which were embroidered the ugliest fiends you can imagine. Horns were blown and drums rolled incessantly. And oh, I forgot to tell you there was also a kind of fiddle, the secret of which is known only to the Shanar priesthood. Its bow is ordinary enough, made of bamboo; but it is whispered that the strings are human veins. . . . When Captain Pole took possession of the priest's body, the priest leaped high in the air, and then rushed on the ox and killed him. He drank off the hot blood, and then began his dance. But what a fright he was when dancing! You know, I am not superstitious. . . . Am I? . . ."

Sham Rao looked at us inquiringly, and I, for one, was glad at this moment that Miss X— was half a mile off, asleep in the *howdah*.

"He turned, and turned, as if possessed by all the demons of Nâraka. The enraged crowd hooted and howled when the priest begun to inflict deep wounds all over his body with the bloody sacrificial knife. To see him, with his hair waving in the wind and his mouth covered with foam; to see him bathing in the blood of the sacrificed animal, mixing it with his own, was more than I could bear. I felt as if hallucinated, I fancied I also was spinning round. . . ."

Sham Rao stopped abruptly, struck dumb. Kangalim stood

before us!

Her appearance was so unexpected that we all felt embarrassed. Carried away by Sham Rao's description, we had noticed neither how nor whence she came. Had she appeared from beneath the earth we could not have been more astonished. Narayan stared at her, opening wide his big jet-black eyes; the *Babu* clicked his tongue in utter confusion.

Imagine a skeleton seven feet high, covered with brown leather, with a dead child's tiny head stuck on its bony shoulders; the eyes set so deep and at the same time flashing such fiendish flames all through your body that you begin to feel your brain stop working, your thoughts become entangled and your blood freeze in your veins.

I describe my personal impressions, and no words of mine can do them justice. My description is too weak. Mr. Y— and the colonel both grew pale under her stare and Mr. Y— made a movement as if about to rise.

Needless to say that such an impression could not last. As soon as the witch had turned her gleaming eyes to the kneeling crowd, it vanished as swiftly as it had come. But still all our attention was fixed on this remarkable creature.

Three hundred years old! Who can tell? Judging by her appearance, we might as well conjecture her to be a thousand. We beheld a genuine living mummy, or rather a mummy endowed with motion. She seemed to have been withering since the creation. Neither time, nor the ills of life, nor the elements could ever affect this living statue of death. The all-destroying hand of time had touched her and stopped short. Time could do no more, and so had left her. And with all this, not a single gray hair. Her long black locks shone with a greenish sheen, and fell in heavy masses down to her knees.

To my great shame, I must confess that a disgusting reminiscence flashed into my memory. I thought about the hair and the nails of corpses growing in the graves, and tried to examine the nails of the old woman.

Meanwhile, she stood motionless as if suddenly transformed into an ugly idol. In one hand she held a dish with a piece of burning camphor, in the other a handful of rice, and she never removed her burning eyes from the crowd. The pale yellow flame of the camphor flickered in the wind, and lit up her death-like head, almost touching her chin; but she paid no heed to it. Her neck, as wrinkled as a mushroom, as thin as a stick, was surrounded by three rows of golden medallions. Her head was adorned with a golden snake. Her grotesque, hardly human body was covered by a piece of saffron-yellow muslin.

The demoniac little girls raised their heads from beneath the leaves, and set up a prolonged animal-like howl. Their example was followed by the old man, who lay exhausted by his frantic dance.

The witch tossed her head convulsively, and began her invocations, rising on tiptoe, as if moved by some external force.

"The goddess, one of the seven sisters, begins to take possession of her," whispered Sham Rao, not even thinking of wiping away the big drops of sweat that streamed from his brow. "Look, look at her!"

This advice was quite superfluous. We *were* looking at her, and at nothing else.

At first, the movements of the witch were slow, unequal, somewhat convulsive; then, gradually, they became less angular; at last, as if catching the cadence of the drums, leaning all her long body forward, and writhing like an eel, she rushed round and round the blazing bonfire. A dry leaf caught in a hurricane could not fly swifter. Her bare bony feet trod noiselessly on the rocky ground. The long locks of her hair flew round her like snakes, lashing the spectators, who knelt, stretching their trembling arms towards her, and writhing as if they were alive. Whoever was touched by one of this Fury's black curls, fell down on the ground, overcome with happiness, shouting thanks to the goddess, and considering himself blessed forever. It was not human hair that touched the happy elect, it was the goddess herself, one of the seven.

Swifter and swifter fly her decrepit legs; the young, vigorous hands of the drummer can hardly follow her. But she does not think of catching the measure of his music; she rushes, she flies forward. Staring with her expressionless, motionless orbs at something before her, at something that is not visible to our mortal eyes, she hardly glances at her worshippers; then her look becomes full of fire, and whoever she looks at feels burned through to the marrow of his bones. At every glance she throws a few grains of rice. The small handful seems inexhaustible, as if the wrinkled palm contained the bottomless bag of Prince Fortunatus.

Suddenly she stops as if thunderstruck.

The mad race round the bonfire had lasted twelve minutes, but we looked in vain for a trace of fatigue on the death-like face of the witch. She stopped only for a moment, just the necessary time for the goddess to release her. As soon as she felt free, by a single effort she jumped over the fire and plunged into the deep tank by the *portico*. This time she plunged only once, and whilst she stayed under the water the second sister-goddess entered her body. The little boy in white produced another dish, with a new piece of burning camphor, just in time for the witch to take it up, and to rush again on her headlong way.

The colonel sat with his watch in his hand. During the second obsession the witch ran, leaped, and raced for exactly fourteen minutes. After this, she plunged twice in the tank, in honor of the second sister; and with every new obsession the number of her plunges increased, till it became six.

It was already an hour and a half since the race began. All this time the witch never rested, stopping only for a few seconds, to disappear under the water.

"She is a fiend, she cannot be a woman!" exclaimed the colonel, seeing the head of the witch immersed for the sixth time in the water.

"Hang me if I know!" grumbled Mr.Y—, nervously pulling his beard. "The only thing I know is that a grain of her cursed rice entered my throat, and I can't get it out!"

"Hush, hush! Please, do be quiet!" implored Sham Rao. "By talking you will spoil the whole business!"

I glanced at Narayan and lost myself in conjectures.

His features, which usually were so calm and serene, were

quite altered at this moment by a deep shadow of suffering. His lips trembled, and the pupils of his eyes were dilated, as if by a dose of *belladonna*. His eyes were lifted over the heads of the crowd, as if in his disgust he tried not to see what was before him, and at the same time could not see it, engaged in a deep reverie which carried him away from us and from the whole performance.

"What is the matter with him?" was my thought, but I had no time to ask him, because the witch was again in full swing, chasing her own shadow.

But with the seventh goddess the program was slightly changed. The running of the old woman changed to leaping. Sometimes bending down to the ground, like a black panther, she leaped up to some worshipper, and halting before him touched his forehead with her finger, while her long, thin body shook with inaudible laughter. Then, again, as if shrinking back playfully from her shadow, and chased by it, in some uncanny game, the witch appeared to us like a horrid caricature of Dinorah, dancing her mad dance. Suddenly she straightened herself to her full height, darted to the *portico* and crouched before the smoking censer, beating her forehead against the granite steps. Another jump, and she was quite close to us, before the head of the monstrous Sivatherium. She knelt down again and bowed her head to the ground several times, with the sound of an empty barrel knocked against something hard.

We had hardly the time to spring to our feet and shrink back when she appeared on the top of the Sivatherium's head, standing there amongst the horns.

Narayan alone did not stir, and fearlessly looked straight in the eyes of the frightful sorceress.

But what was this? Who spoke in those deep manly tones? Her lips were moving, from her breast were issuing those quick, abrupt phrases, but the voice sounded hollow as if coming from beneath the ground.

"Hush, hush!" whispered Sham Rao, his whole body trembling. "She is going to prophesy! .. "

"She?" incredulously inquired Mr. Y—. "This a woman's

voice? I don't believe it for a moment. Someone's uncle must be stowed away somewhere about the place. Not the fabulous uncle she inherited from, but a real live one!. . ."

Sham Rao winced under the irony of this supposition, and cast an imploring look at the speaker.

"Woe to you! woe to you!" echoed the voice. "Woe to you, children of the impure Jaya and Vijaya! of the mocking, unbelieving lingerers round great Shiva's door! Ye, who are cursed by eighty thousand sages Woe to you who believe not in the goddess Kâli, and you who deny us, her seven divine sisters! Flesh-eating, yellow-legged vultures! friends of the oppressors of our land! dogs who are not ashamed to eat from the same trough with the *Bellati!*" (foreigners).

"It seems to me that your prophetess only foretells the past," said Mr.Y—, philosophically putting his hands in his pockets. "I should say that she is hinting at you, my dear Sham Rao."

"Yes! and at us also," murmured the colonel, who was evidently beginning to feel uneasy.

As to the unlucky Sham Rao, he broke out in a cold sweat, and tried to assure us that we were mistaken, that we did not fully understand her language.

"It is not about you, it is not about you! It is of me she speaks, because I am in government service. Oh, she is inexorable!"

"*Râkshasas! Asuras!*" thundered the voice. "How dare you appear before us? how dare you to stand on this holy ground in boots made of a cow's sacred skin? Be cursed for etern———"

But her curse was not destined to be finished. In an instant the Hercules-like Narayan had fallen on the Sivatherium, and upset the whole pile, the skull, the horns and the demoniac Pythia included. A second more, and we thought we saw the witch flying in the air towards the *portico*. A confused vision of a stout, shaven Brahman, suddenly emerging from under the Sivatherium and instantly disappearing in the hollow beneath it, flashed before my dilated eyes.

But, alas! after the third second had passed, we all came to the embarrassing conclusion that, judging from the loud clang of the door of the cave, the representative of the Seven Sisters had ignominiously fled. The moment she had disappeared from our inquisitive eyes to her subterranean domain, we all realized that the unearthly hollow voice we had heard had nothing supernatural about it and belonged to the Brahman hidden under the Sivatherium—to someone's live uncle, as Mr. Y— had rightly supposed.

★★★★★★

Oh, Narayan! how carelessly, how disorderly the worlds rotate around us. I begin to seriously doubt their reality. From this moment I shall earnestly believe that all things in the universe are nothing but illusion, a mere *Mâyâ*. I am becoming a Vedantin.... I doubt that in the whole universe there may be found anything more objective than a Hindu witch flying up the spout.

★★★★★★

Miss X— woke up, and asked what was the meaning of all this noise. The noise of many voices and the sounds of the many retreating footsteps, the general rush of the crowd, had frightened her. She listened to us with a condescending smile, and a few yawns, and went to sleep again.

Next morning, at daybreak, we very reluctantly, it must be owned, bade goodbye to the kind-hearted, good-natured Sham Rao. The confoundingly easy victory of Narayan hung heavily on his mind. His faith in the holy hermitess and the seven goddesses was a good deal shaken by the shameful capitulation of the sisters, who had surrendered at the first blow from a mere mortal. But during the dark hours of the night he had had time to think it over, and to shake off the uneasy feeling of having unwillingly misled and disappointed his European friends.

Sham Rao still looked confused when he shook hands with us at parting, and expressed to us the best wishes of his family and himself.

As to the heroes of this truthful narrative, they mounted their elephants once more, and directed their heavy steps towards the high road and Jubbulpore.

The Legend of the Blue Lotus

Century after century has passed away since Ambarisha, King of Ayodhya, reigned in the city founded by the holy Manu, Vaivasvata, the offspring of the Sun. The king was a Suryavansi (a descendant of the Solar Race), and he avowed himself a most faithful servant of the God, Varuna, the greatest and most powerful deity in the Rig-Veda.

★★★★★★

It is only much later in the orthodox Pantheon and the symbolical polytheism of the Brahmans that Varuna became Poseidon or Neptune—which he is now. In the Vedas he is the most ancient of the Gods, identical with Ouranos of the Greek, that is to say a personification of the celestial space and the infinite gods, the creator and ruler of heaven and earth, the King, the Father and the Master of the world, of gods and of men. Hesiod's Uranus and the Greek Zeus are one.

★★★★★★

But the god had denied male heirs to his worshipper, and this made the king very unhappy.

"Alas!" he wailed, every morning while performing his *puja* to the lesser gods, "alas! What avails it to be the greatest king on earth when God denies me an heir of my blood. When I am dead and placed on the funeral pyre, who will fulfil the pious duties of a son, and shatter my lifeless skull to liberate my soul from its earthly trammels? What strange hand will at the full moon-tide place the rice of the *Shraddha* ceremony to do reverence to my shade? Will not the very birds of death (Rooks and ravens) themselves turn from the funeral feast? For, surely, my shade earthbound in its great despair will not permit them to partake of it."

★★★★★★

The *Shradda* is a ceremony observed by the nearest relatives of the deceased for the nine days following the death. Once upon a time it

153

was a magical ceremony. Now, however, in addition to other practices, it mainly consists of scattering balls of cooked rice before the door of the dead man's house. If the crows promptly eat the rice it is a sign that the soul is liberated and at rest. If these birds which are so greedy did not touch the food, it was a proof that the *pisacha* or *bhut* (shade) is present and is preventing them. Undoubtedly the *Shradda* is a superstition, but certainly not more so than Novenas or masses for the Dead.

★★★★★★

The king was thus bewailing, when his family priest inspired him with the idea of making a vow. If God should send him two or more sons, he would promise God to sacrifice to Him at a public ceremony the eldest born when he should have attained the age of puberty.

Attracted by this promise of a burnt-offering of flesh—a savoury odour very agreeable to the Great Gods—Varuna accepted the promise of the king, and the happy Ambarisha had a son, followed by several others. The eldest son, the heir to the throne for the time being, was called Rohita (the red) and was surnamed Devarata—which, literally translated, means God-given. Devarata grew up and soon became a veritable Prince Charming, but if we are to believe the legends he was as selfish and deceitful as he was beautiful.

When the prince had attained the appointed age, the God speaking through the mouth of the same Court Priest, charged the king to keep his promise; but when each time Ambarisha invented some excuse to postpone the hour of sacrifice, the God at last grew annoyed. Being a jealous and angry God, he threatened the king with all His Divine wrath.

For a long time, neither commands nor threats produced the desired effect. As long as there were sacred cows to be transferred from the royal cowsheds to those of the Brahmans, as long as there was money in the Treasury to fill the Temple crypts, the Brahmans succeeded in keeping Varuna quiet. But when there were no more cows, when there was no more money, the God threatened to overthrow the king, his palace and his heirs, and if they escaped, to burn them alive. The poor king, finding himself at the end of his resources, summoned his first-born and informed him of the fate which awaited him. But Devarata lent a deaf ear to these tidings. He refused to submit to the double weight of the paternal and divine will.

So, when the sacrificial fires had been lighted and all the good towns-folk of Ayodhya had gathered together, full of emotion, the heir-apparent was absent from the festival.

He had concealed himself in the forests of the Yogis.

Now, these forests had been inhabited by holy hermits, and Devarata knew that there he would be unassailable and impregnable. He might be seen there, but no one could do him violence—not even the God Varuna Himself. It was a simple solution. The religious austerities of the Aranyakas (the holy men of the forests) several of whom were Daityas (Titans, a race of giants and demons), gave them such dominance that all the Gods trembled before their sway and their supernatural powers—even Varuna, himself.

These antediluvian Yogis, it seems, had the power to destroy even the God Himself, at will—possibly because they had invented Him themselves.

Devarata spent several years in the forests; at last he grew tired of the life. Allowing it to be understood that he could satisfy Varuna by finding a substitute, who would sacrifice himself in his place, provided that the sacrificial victim was the son of a Rishi, he started on his journey and finally discovered that he sought.

In the country which lies around the flower-covered shores of the renowned Pushkara, there was once a famine, and a very holy man, named Ajigarta, (Others call him Rishika and call King Ambarisha, Harischandra, the famous sovereign who was a paragon of all the virtues), was at the point of death from starvation, likewise all his family. He had several sons of whom the second, Sunahsepha, a virtuous young man, was himself also preparing to become a Rishi. Taking advantage of his poverty and thinking with good reason that a hungry stomach would be a more ready listener than a satisfied one, the crafty Devarata made the father acquainted with his history. After this he offered him a hundred cows in exchange for Sunahsepha, a substitute burnt-offering on the altar of the Gods.

The virtuous father refused at first point-blank, but the gentle Sunahsepha offered himself of his own accord, and thus addressed his father: "Of what importance is the life of one man, when it can save that of many others. This God is a great god and His pity is infinite; but He is also a very jealous god and His wrath is swift and vengeful. Varuna is the Lord of Terror, and Death is obedient to His command. His spirit will not for ever strive with one who is disobedient to Him. He will repent Him that He has created man, and then will burn alive a hundred thousand *lakhs* (*lakh* is a measure of 100,000, whether men or pieces of money be in question), of innocent people because of one man who is guilty. If His victim should escape Him, He will surely dry up our rivers, set fire to our lands and destroy our women who are with child—in His infinite kindness. Let me then sacrifice myself, oh! my father, in place of this stranger who offers us a hundred cows. That sum would prevent thee and my brothers from dying of hunger and will save thousands of others from a terrible death. At this price the giving up of life is a pleasant thing."

The aged Rishi shed some tears, but he ended by giving his consent and began to prepare the sacrificial pyre.

★★★★★★

Manu (Book X, 105) alluding to this story remarks that Ajigarta, the holy Rishi, committed no sin in selling the life of his son, since the sacrifice preserved his life and that of all the family. This reminds us of another legend, more modern, that might serve as a parallel to the older one. Did not the Count Ugolino, condemned to die of starvation in his dungeon, eat his own children "to preserve for them a father"? The popular legend of Sunahsepha is more beautiful than the commentary of Manu—evidently an interpolation of some Brahmans in falsified manuscripts.

★★★★★★

The Pushkara Lake was one of the spots of this earth favoured by the Goddess, Lakshmi-Padma (White Lotus); she often plunged into the fresh waters that she might visit her eldest sister, Varuni, the consort of the God Varuna.

★★★★★★

This lake is sometimes called in our day *Pokker*. It is a place famous for a yearly pilgrimage, and is charmingly situated five English miles from Ajmeer in Rajisthan. Pushkara means "the Blue Lotus", the surface of the lake being covered as with a carpet with these beautiful plants. But the legend avers that they were at first white. Pushkara is also the proper name of a man, and the name of one of the "seven sacred islands" in the geography of the Hindus, the *septa dwipa*.

Varuni, Goddess of Heat (later Goddess of Wine) was also born of the Ocean of Milk. Of the "fourteen precious objects" produced by the churning, she appeared the second and Lakshmi the last, preceded by the Chalice of Anmita, the nectar which gives immortality.

★★★★★★

The altar was set up on the shore of the lake, the pyre was prepared and the crowd had assembled. After he had laid his son on the perfumed sandal wood and bound him, Ajigarta equipped himself with the knife of sacrifice. He was just raising his trembling arm above the

156

heart of his well-beloved son, when the boy began to chant the sacred verses. There was again a moment of hesitation and supreme grief, and as the boy finished his mantram, the aged Rishi plunged his knife into the breast of Sunahsepha.

Lakshmi-Padma heard the proposal of Devarata, witnessed the despair of the father, and admired the filial devotion of Sunahsepha. Filled with pity, the Mother of Love and Compassion sent for the Rishi Visvamitra, one of the seven primordial Manus and a son of Brahma, and succeeded in interesting him in the lot of her *protégé*. The great Rishi promised her his aid. Appearing to Sunahsepha, but unseen by all others, he taught him two sacred verses (mantras) of the *Rig-Veda*, making him promise to recite these on the pyre. Now, he who utters these two mantras (invocations) forces the whole assembly of the Gods, with Indra at their head, to come to his rescue, and because of this becomes a Rishi himself in this life or in his next incarnation.

But, oh! the miracle of it! At that very moment Indra, the God of the Blue Vault (the Universe) issued from the heavens and descended right into the midst of the ceremony. Enveloping the pyre and the victim in a thick blue mist, he loosed the ropes which held the youth captive. It seemed as if a corner of the azure heavens had lowered itself over the spot, illuminating the whole country and colouring with a golden blue the whole scene. Filled with terror, the crowd, and even the Rishi himself, fell on their faces, half dead with fear.

When they came to themselves, the mist had disappeared and a complete change of scene had been wrought.

The fires of the funeral pyre had rekindled of themselves, and stretched thereon was seen a hind (Rohit) which was none else than the Prince Rohita, Devarata, who, pierced to the heart with the knife he had directed against another, was burning as a sacrifice for his sin.

★★★★★★

A play upon words. *Rohit* in Sanskrit is the Dame of the female of the deer, the hind, and *Rohita* means "red". It was because of his cowardice and fear of death that he was changed, according to the legend, into a hind by the Gods.

★★★★★★

Some little way apart from the altar, also lying stretched out, but on a bed of Lotuses, peacefully slept Sunahsepha; and in the place on his breast where the knife had descended was seen to bloom a beautiful blue lotus. The Pushkara Lake, itself, covered a moment before with

157

white lotuses, whose petals shone in the sun like silver cups full of Amrita's waters, (the elixir which confers immortality), now reflected the azure of the heavens—the white lotuses had become blue.

Then like to the sound of the Vina, (type of lute, invention of which is attributed to Shiva), rising to the air from the depth of the waters, was heard a melodious voice which uttered these words and this curse:

A prince who does not know how to die for his subjects is not worthy to reign over the children of the Sun. He will be reborn in a race of red-haired peoples, a barbarous and selfish race, and the nations which descend from him will have a heritage ever on the decline. It is the younger son of a mendicant ascetic who will become the king and reign in his stead.

A murmur of approbation set in movement the flowery carpet that overspread the lake. Opening to the golden sunlight their hearts of blue, the lotuses smiled with joy and wafted a hymn of perfume to Surya, their Sun and Master. All nature rejoiced, save Devarata, who was but a handful of ashes.

Then Visvamitra, the great Rishi, although he was already the father of a hundred sons, adopted Sunahsepha as his eldest son and as a precautionary measure cursed in advance anyone who should refuse to recognise, in the last born of the Rishi, the eldest of his children and the legitimate heir of the throne of Ambarisha.

Because of this decree, Sunahsepha was born in his next incarnation in the royal family of Ayodha and reigned over the Solar race for 84,000 years.

With regard to Rohita—Devarata or God-given as he was—he fulfilled the lot which Lakshmi Padma had vowed. He reincarnated in the family of a foreigner without caste (Mleccha-Yavana) and became the ancestor of the barbarous and red-haired races which dwell in the West.

★★★★★★

It is for the conversion of these races that the *Lotus Bleu* has been established.

If any of our readers should allow themselves to doubt the historical truth of this adventure of our ancestor; Rohita, and of the transformation of the white lotus into the blue lotus, they are invited to make a journey to Ajmeer.

Once there, they need only to go to the shores of the lake thrice blessed, named Pushkara, where every pilgrim who bathes during the full moon time of the month of Krhktika (October-November) attains to the highest sanctity, without other effort. There the sceptics would see with their own eyes the site where was built the pyre of Rohita, and also the waters visited by Lakshmi in days of yore.

They might even have seen the blue lotuses, if most of these had not since been changed, thanks to a new transformation decreed by the Gods, into sacred crocodiles which no one has the right to disturb. It is this transformation which gives to nine out of every ten pilgrims who plunge into the waters of the lake, the opportunity of entering into Nirvana almost immediately, and also causes the holy crocodiles to be the most bulky of their kind.

Karmic Visions

(written under the pen name "Sanjna")

Oh, sad no more! Oh, sweet No more!
Oh, strange No more!
By a mossed brook bank on a stone
I smelt a wild weed-flower alone;
There was a ringing in my ears,
And both my eyes gushed out with tears,
Surely all pleasant things had gone before,
Low buried fathom deep beneath with thee, NO MORE.
—Tennyson *The Gem*

1

A camp filled with war-chariots, neighing horses and legions of long-haired soldiers . . .

A regal tent, gaudy in its barbaric splendour. Its linen walls are weighed down under the burden of arms. In its centre a raised seat covered with skins, and on it a stalwart, savage-looking warrior. He passes in review prisoners of war brought in turn before him, who are disposed of according to the whim of the heartless despot.

A new captive is now before him, and is addressing him with passionate earnestness . . . As he listens to her with suppressed passion in his manly, but fierce, cruel face, the balls of his eyes become bloodshot and roll with fury. And as he bends forward with fierce stare, his whole appearance—his matted locks hanging over the frowning brow, his big-boned body with strong sinews, and the two large hands resting on the shield placed upon the right knee—justifies the remark made in hardly audible whisper by a grey-headed soldier to his neighbour:

Little mercy shall the holy prophetess receive at the hands of Clovis!

The captive, who stands between two Burgundian warriors, facing the ex-prince of the Salians, now king of all the Franks, is an old woman with silver-white dishevelled hair, hanging over her skeleton-like shoulders. In spite of her great age, her tall figure is erect; and the inspired black eyes look proudly and fearlessly into the cruel face of the treacherous son of Gilderich.

"Aye, King," she says, in a loud, ringing voice. "Aye, thou art great and mighty now, but thy days are numbered, and thou shalt reign but three summers longer. Wicked thou wert born . . . perfidious thou art to thy friends and allies, robbing more than one of his lawful crown. Murderer of thy next-of-kin, thou who addest to the knife and spear in open warfare, dagger, poison and treason, beware how thou dearest with the servant of Nerthus!" (*The Nourishing* (Tacit. Germ. XI)—the Earth, a Mother-Goddess, the most beneficent deity of the ancient Germans).

"Ha, ha, ha! . . . old hag of Hell!" chuckles the king, with an evil, ominous sneer. "Thou hast crawled out of the entrails of thy mother-goddess truly. Thou fearest not my wrath? It is well. But little need I fear thine empty imprecations . . . I, a baptised Christian!"

"So, so," replies the Sybil. "All know that Clovis has abandoned the gods of his fathers; that he has lost all faith in the warning voice of the white horse of the Sun, and that out of fear of the Allimani he went serving on his knees Remigius, the servant of the Nazarene, at Rheims. But hast thou become any truer in thy new faith? Hast thou not murdered in cold blood all thy brethren who trusted in thee, after, as well as before, thy apostasy? Hast not thou plighted troth to Alaric, the King of the West Goths, and hast thou not killed him by stealth, running thy spear into his back while he was bravely fighting an enemy? And is it thy new faith and thy new gods that teach thee to be devising in thy black soul even now foul means against Theodoric, who put thee down? . . . Beware, Clovis, beware! For now the gods of thy fathers have risen against thee! Beware, I say, for . . . "

"Woman!" fiercely cries the king—"Woman, cease thy insane talk and answer my question. Where is the treasure of the grove amassed by thy priests of Satan, and hidden after they had been driven away by the Holy Cross? . . . Thou alone knowest. Answer, or by Heaven and Hell I shall thrust thy evil tongue down thy throat for ever!" . . .

She heeds not the threat, but goes on calmly and fearlessly as before, as if she had not heard.

"The gods say, Clovis, thou art accursed Clovis, thou shalt be reborn among thy present enemies, and suffer the tortures thou hast inflicted upon thy victims. All the combined power and glory thou hast deprived them of shall be thine in prospect, yet thou shalt never reach it! . . . Thou shalt . . . ."

The prophetess never finishes her sentence.

With a terrible oath the king, crouching like a wild beast on his skin-covered seat, pounces upon her with the leap of a jaguar, and with one blow fells her to the ground. And as he lifts his sharp murderous spear the "Holy One" of the Sun-worshipping tribe makes the air ring with a last imprecation.

"I curse thee, enemy of Nerthus! May my agony be tenfold thine! . . . May the Great Law avenge. . . ."

The heavy spear falls, and, running through the victim's throat, nails the head to the ground. A stream of hot crimson blood gushes from the gaping wound and covers king and soldiers with indelible gore . . .

2

Time—the landmark of gods and men in the boundless field of Eternity, the murderer of its offspring and of memory in mankind—time moves on with noiseless, incessant step through aeons and ages. Among millions of other Souls, a Soul-Ego is reborn: for weal or for woe, who knoweth! Captive in its new human Form, it grows with it, and together they become, at last, conscious of their existence.

Happy are the years of their blooming youth, unclouded with want or sorrow. Neither knows aught of the Past nor of the Future. For them all is the joyful Present: for the Soul-Ego is unaware that it had ever lived in other human tabernacles, it knows not that it shall be again reborn, and it takes no thought of the morrow.

Its Form is calm and content. It has hitherto given its Soul-Ego no heavy troubles. Its happiness is due to the continuous mild serenity of its temper, to the affection it spreads wherever it goes. For it is a noble Form, and its heart is full of benevolence. Never has the Form startled its Soul-Ego with a too-violent shock, or otherwise disturbed the calm placidity of its tenant.

Two score of years glide by like one short pilgrimage; a long walk through the sunlit paths of life, hedged by ever-blooming roses with no thorns. The rare sorrows that befall the twin pair, Form and Soul, appear to them rather like the pale light of the cold northern moon, whose beams throw into a deeper shadow all around the moon-lit objects, than as the blackness of the night, the night of hopeless sorrow and despair.

Son of a prince, born to rule himself one day his father's kingdom; surrounded from his cradle by reverence and honours; deserving of the universal respect and sure of the love of all—what could the Soul-Ego desire more for the Form it dwelt in.

And so, the Soul-Ego goes on enjoying existence in its tower of strength, gazing quietly at the panorama of life ever changing before its two windows—the two kind blue eyes of a loving and good man.

3

One day an arrogant and boisterous enemy threatens the father's kingdom, and the savage instincts of the warrior of old awaken in the Soul-Ego. It leaves its dreamland amid the blossoms of life and causes its Ego of clay to draw the soldier's blade, assuring him it is in defence of his country.

Prompting each other to action, they defeat the enemy and cover themselves with glory and pride. They make the haughty foe bite the dust at their feet in supreme humiliation. For this they are crowned by history with the unfading laurels of valour, which are those of success. They make a footstool of the fallen enemy and transform their sire's little kingdom into a great empire. Satisfied they could achieve no more for the present, they return to seclusion and to the dreamland of their sweet home.

For three lustra more the Soul-Ego sits at its usual post, beaming out of its windows on the world around. Over its head the sky is blue and the vast horizons are covered with those seemingly unfading flowers that grow in the sunlight of health and strength. All looks fair as a verdant mead in spring . . .

4

But an evil day comes to all in the drama of being. It waits through the life of king and of beggar. It leaves traces on the history of every mortal born from woman, and it can neither be seared away, entreated, nor propitiated. Health is a dewdrop that falls from the heavens to vivify the blossoms on earth, only during the morn'. of life, its spring and summer . . . It has but a short duration and returns from whence it came—the invisible realms.

How oft 'neath the bud that is brightest and fairest,
The seeds of the canker in embryo lurk!

How oft at the root of the flower that is rarest —
Secure in its ambush the worm is at work. . . . . .

The running sand which moves downward in the glass, wherein the hours of human life are numbered, runs swifter. The worm has gnawed the blossom of health through its heart. The strong body is found stretched one day on the thorny bed of pain.

The Soul-Ego beams no longer. It sits still and looks sadly out of what has become its dungeon windows, on the world which is now rapidly being shrouded for it in the funeral palls of suffering. Is it the eve of night eternal which is nearing?

5

Beautiful are the resorts on the midland sea. An endless line of surf-beaten, black, rugged rocks stretches, hemmed in between the golden sands of the coast and the deep blue waters of the gulf. They offer their granite breast to the fierce blows of the north-west wind and thus protect the dwellings of the rich that nestle at their foot on the inland side. The half-ruined cottages on the open shore are the insufficient shelter of the poor. Their squalid bodies are often crushed under the walls torn and washed down by wind and angry wave. But they only follow the great law of the survival of the fittest. Why should *they* be protected?

Lovely is the morning when the sun dawns with golden amber tints and its first rays kiss the cliffs of the beautiful shore. Glad is the song of the lark, as, emerging from its warm nest of herbs, it drinks the morning dew from the deep flower-cups; when the tip of the rosebud thrills under the caress of the first sunbeam, and earth and heaven smile in mutual greeting. Sad is the Soul-Ego alone as it gazes on awakening nature from the high couch opposite the large bay-window.

How calm is the approaching noon as the shadow creeps steadily on the sundial towards the hour of rest! Now the hot sun begins to melt the clouds in the limpid air and the last shreds of the morning mist that lingers on the tops of the distant hills vanish in it. All nature is prepared to rest at the hot and lazy hour of midday. The feathered tribes cease their song; their soft, gaudy wings droop and they hang their drowsy heads, seeking refuge from the burning heat. A morning lark is busy nestling in the bordering bushes under the clustering flowers of the pomegranate and the sweet bay of the Mediterranean. The active songster has become voiceless.

"Its voice will resound as joyfully again tomorrow!" sighs the Soul-

Ego, as it listens to the dying buzzing of the insects on the verdant turf. "Shall ever mine?"

And now the flower-scented breeze hardly stirs the languid heads of the luxuriant plants. A solitary palm-tree, growing out of the cleft of a moss-covered rock, next catches the eye of the Soul-Ego. Its once upright, cylindrical trunk has been twisted out of shape and half-broken by the nightly blasts of the north-west winds. And as it stretches wearily its drooping feathery arms, swayed to and fro in the blue pellucid air, its body trembles and threatens to break in two at the first new gust that may arise.

"And then, the severed part will fall into the sea, and the once stately palm will be no more," soliloquizes the Soul-Ego as it gazes sadly out of its windows.

Everything returns to life, in the cool, old bower at the hour of sunset. The shadows on the sun-dial become with every moment thicker, and animate nature awakens busier than ever in the cooler hours of approaching night. Birds and insects chirrup and buzz their last evening hymns around the tall and still powerful Form, as it paces slowly and wearily along the gravel walk. And now its heavy gaze falls wistfully on the azure bosom of the tranquil sea. The gulf sparkles like a gem-studded carpet of blue-velvet in the farewell dancing sunbeams, and smiles like a thoughtless, drowsy child, weary of tossing about. Further on, calm and serene in its perfidious beauty, the open sea stretches far and wide the smooth mirror of its cool waters—salt and bitter as human tears. It lies in its treacherous repose like a gorgeous, sleeping monster, watching over the unfathomed mystery of its dark abysses. Truly the monumentless cemetry of the millions sunk in its depths . . .

Without a grave,
Unknell'd, uncoffined and unknown . . . .

while the sorry relic of the once noble Form pacing yonder, once that its hour strikes and the deep-voiced bells toll the knell for the departed soul, shall be laid out in state and pomp. Its dissolution will be announced by millions of trumpet voices. Kings, princes and the mighty ones of the earth will be present at its obsequies, or will send their representatives with sorrowful faces and condoling messages to those left behind . . .

"*One point gained, over those 'uncoffined and unknown',*" is the bitter reflection of the Soul-Ego.

Thus, glides past one day after the other; and as swift-winged Time urges his flight, every vanishing hour destroying some thread in the tissue of life, the Soul-Ego is gradually transformed in its views of things and men. Flitting between two eternities, far away from its birthplace, solitary among its crowd of physicians, and attendants, the Form is drawn with every day nearer to its Spirit-Soul. Another light unapproached and unapproachable in days of joy, softly descends upon the weary prisoner. It sees now that which it had never perceived before. . . .

6

How grand, how mysterious are the spring nights on the seashore when the winds are chained and the elements lulled! A solemn silence reigns in nature. Alone the silvery, scarcely audible ripple of the wave, as it runs caressingly over the moist sand, kissing shells and pebbles on its up and down journey, reaches the ear like the regular soft breathing of a sleeping bosom. How small, how insignificant and helpless feels man, during these quiet hours, as he stands between the two gigantic magnitudes, the star-hung dome above, and the slumbering earth below. Heaven and earth are plunged in sleep, but their souls are awake, and they confabulate, whispering one to the other mysteries unspeakable.

It is then that the occult side of Nature lifts her dark veils for us, and reveals secrets we would vainly seek to extort from her during the day. The firmament, so distant, so far away from earth, now seems to approach and bend over her. The sidereal meadows exchange embraces with their more humble sisters of the earth—the daisy-decked valleys and the green slumbering fields. The heavenly dome falls prostrate into the arms of the great quiet sea; and the millions of stars that stud the former peep into and bathe in every lakelet and pool. To the grief-furrowed soul those twinkling orbs are the eyes of angels. They look down with ineffable pity on the suffering of mankind. It is not the night dew that falls on the sleeping flowers, but sympathetic tears that drop from those orbs, at the sight of the *great human sorrow* . . .

Yes; sweet and beautiful is a southern night. But—
When silently we watch the bed, by the taper is flickering light,
When all we love is fading fast—how terrible is night. . . .

7

Another day is added to the series of buried days. The far green hills, and the fragrant boughs of the pomegranate blossom have melted in the mellow shadows of the night, and both sorrow and joy are plunged in the lethargy of soul-resting sleep. Every noise has died out in the royal gardens, and no voice or sound is heard in that overpowering stillness.

Swift-winged dreams descend from the laughing stars in motley crowds, and landing upon the earth disperse among mortals and immortals, amid animals and men. They hover over the sleepers, each attracted by its affinity and kind; dreams of joy and hope, balmy and innocent visions, terrible and awesome sights seen with sealed eyes, sensed by the soul; some instilling happiness and consolation, others causing sobs to heave the sleeping bosoms, tears and mental torture, all and one preparing unconsciously to the sleepers their waking thoughts of the morrow.

Even in sleep the Soul-Ego finds no rest.

Hot and feverish its body tosses about in restless agony. For it, the time of happy dreams is now a vanished shadow, a long bygone recollection. Through the mental agony of the soul, there lies a transformed man. Through the physical agony of the frame, there flutters in it a fully awakened Soul. The veil of illusion has fallen off from the cold idols of the world, and the vanities and emptiness of fame and wealth stand bare, often hideous, before its eyes. The thoughts of the Soul fall like dark shadows on the cogitative faculties of the fast disorganizing body, haunting the thinker daily, nightly, hourly . . .

The sight of his snorting steed pleases him no longer. The recollections of guns and banners wrested from the enemy; of cities razed, of trenches, cannons and tents, of an array of conquered spoils now stirs but little his national pride. Such thoughts move him no more, and ambition has become powerless to awaken in his aching heart the haughty recognition of any valorous deed of chivalry. Visions of another kind now haunt his weary days and long sleepless nights . . .

What he now sees is a throng of bayonets clashing against each other in a mist of smoke and blood; thousands of mangled corpses covering the ground, torn and cut to shreds by the murderous weapons devised by science and civilization, blessed to success by the servants of his God. What he now dreams of are bleeding, wounded and dying men, with missing limbs and matted locks, wet and soaked through with gore . . .

8

A hideous dream detaches itself from a group of passing visions, and alights heavily on his aching chest. The nightmare shows him men expiring on the battlefield with a curse on those who led them to their destruction. Every pang in his own wasting body brings to him in dream the recollection of pangs still worse, of pangs suffered through and for him. He sees and *feels* the torture of the fallen millions, who die after long hours of terrible mental and physical agony; who expire in forest and plain, in stagnant ditches by the road-side, in pools of blood under a sky made black with smoke. His eyes are once more riveted to the torrents of blood, every drop of which represents a tear of despair, a heart-rent cry, a lifelong sorrow.

He hears again the thrilling sighs of desolation, and the shrill cries ringing through mount, forest and valley. He sees the old mothers who have lost the light of their souls; families, the hand that fed them. He beholds widowed young wives thrown on the wide, cold world, and beggared orphans wailing in the streets by the thousands. He finds the young daughters of his bravest old soldiers exchanging their mourning garments for the gaudy frippery of prostitution, and the Soul-Ego shudders in the sleeping Form. . . His heart is rent by the groans of the famished; his eyes blinded by the smoke of burning hamlets, of homes destroyed, of towns and cities in smouldering ruins. . . .

And in his terrible dream, he remembers that moment of insanity in his soldier's life, when standing over a heap of the dead and the dying, waving in his right hand a naked sword red to its hilt with smoking blood, and in his left, the colours rent from the hand of the warrior expiring at his feet, he had sent in a stentorian voice praises to the throne of the Almighty, thanksgiving for the victory just obtained! . . .

He starts in his sleep and awakes in horror. A great shudder shakes his frame like an aspen leaf, and sinking back on his pillows, sick at the recollection, he hears a voice—the voice of the Soul-Ego—saying in him:

Fame and victory are vainglorious words . . . Thanksgiving and prayers for lives destroyed—wicked lies and blasphemy! . . .

The Soul in him whispers:

What have they brought thee or to thy fatherland, those bloody victories!

It replies. . . .

A population clad in iron armour. Two score millions of men dead now to all spiritual aspiration and Soul-life. A people, henceforth deaf to the peaceful voice of the honest citizen's duty, averse to a life of peace, blind to the arts and literature, indifferent to all but lucre and ambition. What is thy future Kingdom, now? A legion of war-puppets as units, a great wild beast in their collectivity. A beast that, like the sea yonder, slumbers gloomily now, but to fall with the more fury on the first enemy that is indicated to it. Indicated, by whom? It is as though a heartless, proud Fiend, assuming sudden authority, incarnate Ambition and Power, had clutched with iron hand the minds of a whole country. By what wicked enchantment has he brought the people back to those primeval days of the nation when their ancestors, the yellow-haired Suevi, and the treacherous Franks roamed about in their war-like spirit, thirsting to kill, to decimate and subject each other.

By what infernal powers has this been accomplished? Yet the transformation has been produced and it is as undeniable as the fact that alone the Fiend rejoices and boasts of the transformation effected. The whole world is hushed in breathless expectation. Not a wife or mother, but is haunted in her dreams by the black and ominous storm-cloud that overhangs the whole of Europe. The cloud is approaching It comes nearer and nearer. . . Oh woe and horror! . . . . I foresee once more for earth the suffering I have already witnessed. I read the fatal destiny upon the brow of the flower of Europe's youth! But if I live and have the power, never, oh never shall my country take part in it again! No, no, I will not see—

The glutton death gorged with devouring lives. . . .
I will not hear —
robb'd mother's shrieks
While from men's piteous wounds and horrid gashes
The lab'ring life flows faster than the blood! . . . .

9

Firmer and firmer grows in the Soul-Ego the feeling of intense hatred for the terrible butchery called war; deeper and deeper does it impress its thoughts upon the Form that holds it captive. Hope awakens at times in the aching breast and colours the long hours of solitude and meditation; like the morning ray that dispels the dusky shades of shadowy despondency, it lightens the long hours of lonely thought. But as the rainbow is not always the dispeller of the storm-clouds but often only a refraction of the setting sun on a passing cloud, so the moments of dreamy hope are generally followed by hours of still blacker despair. Why, oh why, thou mocking Nemesis, hast thou thus purified and enlightened, among all the sovereigns on this earth, him, whom thou hast made helpless, speechless and powerless? Why hast thou kindled the flame of holy brotherly love for man in the breast of one whose heart already feels the approach of the icy hand of death and decay, whose strength is steadily deserting him and whose very life is melting away like foam on the crest of a breaking wave?

And now the hand of Fate is upon the couch of pain. The hour for the fulfilment of nature's law has struck at last. The old Sire is no more; the younger man is henceforth a monarch. Voiceless and helpless, he is nevertheless a potentate, the autocratic master of millions of subjects. Cruel Fate has erected a throne for him over an open grave, and beckons him to glory and to power. Devoured by suffering, he finds himself suddenly crowned. The wasted Form is snatched from its warm nest amid the palm groves and the roses; it is whirled from balmy south to the frozen north, where waters harden into crystal groves and "waves on waves in solid mountains rise"; whither he now speeds to reign and—speeds to die.

10

Onward, onward rushes the black, fire-vomiting monster, devised by man to partially conquer Space and Time. Onward, and further with every moment from the health-giving, balmy South flies the train. Like the Dragon of the Fiery Head, it devours distance and leaves behind it a long trail of smoke, sparks and stench. And as its long, tortuous, flexible body, wriggling and hissing like a gigantic dark reptile, glides swiftly, crossing mountain and moor, forest, tunnel and plain, its swinging monotonous motion lulls the worn-out occupant, the weary and heartsore Form, to sleep . . .

In the moving palace the air is warm and balmy. The luxurious vehicle is full of exotic plants; and from a large cluster of sweet-smelling flowers arises together with its scent the fairy queen of dreams, followed by her band of joyous elves. The Dryads laugh in their leafy bowers as the train glides by, and send floating upon the breeze dreams of green solitudes and fairy visions. The rumbling noise of wheels is gradually transformed into the roar of a distant waterfall, to subside into the silvery trills of a crystalline brook. The Soul-Ego takes its flight into Dreamland. . . .

It travels through aeons of time, and lives, and feels, and breathes under the most contrasted forms and personages. It is now a giant, a Yotun, who rushes into Muspelheim, where Surtur rules with his flaming sword.

It battles fearlessly against a host of monstrous animals, and puts them to fight with a single wave of its mighty hand. Then it sees itself in the Northern Mistworld, it penetrates under the guise of a brave bowman into Helheim, the Kingdom of the Dead, where a Black-Elf reveals to him a series of its lives and their mysterious concatenation. "Why does man suffer?" enquiries the Soul-Ego. "Because he would become one," is the mocking answer. Forthwith, the Soul-Ego stands in the presence of the holy goddess, Saga. She sings to it of the valorous deeds of the Germanic heroes, of their virtues and their vices. She shows the Soul the mighty warriors fallen by the hands of many of its past Forms, on battlefield, as also in the sacred security of home.

It sees itself under the personages of maidens, and of women, of young and old men, and of children. . . . It feels itself dying more than once in those Forms. It expires as a hero—Spirit, and is led by the pitying Walkyries from the bloody battlefield back to the abode of Bliss under the shining foliage of Walhalla. It heaves its last sigh in another form, and is hurled on to the cold, hopeless plane of remorse. It closes its innocent eyes in its last sleep, as an infant, and is forthwith carried along by the beauteous Elves of Light into another body—the doomed generator of Pain and Suffering. In each case the mists of death are dispersed, and pass from the eyes of the Soul-Ego, no sooner does it cross the Black Abyss that separates the Kingdom of the Living from the Realm of the Dead. Thus "Death" becomes but a meaningless word for it, a vain sound. In every instance the beliefs of the Mortal take objective life and shape for the Immortal, as soon as it spans the Bridge. Then they begin to fade, and disappear. . . .

"What is my Past?" enquires the Soul-Ego of Urd, the eldest of the Norn sisters. "Why do I suffer?"

A long parchment is unrolled in her hand, and reveals a long series of mortal beings, in each of whom the Soul-Ego recognises one of its dwellings. When it comes to the last but one, it sees a blood-stained hand doing endless deeds of cruelty and treachery, and it shudders. . . . . Guileless victims arise around it, and cry to Orlog for vengeance.

"What is my immediate Present?" asks the dismayed Soul of Werdandi, the second sister.

"The decree of Orlog is on thyself!" is the answer. "But Orlog does not pronounce them blindly, as foolish mortals have it."

"What is my Future?" asks despairingly of Skuld, the third Norn sister, the Soul-Ego. "Is it to be for ever dark with tears, and bereaved of Hope?" . . .

No answer is received. But the Dreamer feels whirled through space, and suddenly the scene changes. The Soul-Ego finds itself on a, to it, long familiar spot, the royal bower, and the seat opposite the broken palm-tree. Before it stretches, as formerly, the vast blue expanse of waters, glassing the rocks and cliffs; there, too, is the lonely palm, doomed to quick disappearance.

The soft mellow voice of the incessant ripple of the light waves now assumes human speech, and reminds the Soul-Ego of the vows formed more than once on that spot. And the Dreamer repeats with enthusiasm the words pronounced before.

Never, oh, never shall I, henceforth, sacrifice vainglorious fame or ambition a single son of my motherland! Our world is so full of unavoidable misery, so poor with joys and bliss, and shall I add to its cup of bitterness the fathomless ocean of woe and blood, called *war*? *Avaunt*, such thought! . . . Oh, never more. . .

11

Strange sight and change. . . . The broken palm which stands before the mental sight of the Soul-Ego suddenly lifts up its drooping trunk and becomes erect and verdant as before. Still greater bliss, the Soul-Ego finds himself as strong and as healthy as he ever was. In a stentorian voice he sings to the four winds a loud and a joyous song. He feels a wave of joy and bliss in him, and seems to know why he is happy.

He is suddenly transported into what looks a fairy-like Hall, lit with most glowing lights and built of materials, the like of which he had never seen before. He perceives the heirs and descendants of all the monarchs of the globe gathered in that Hall in one happy family. They wear no longer the insignia of royalty, but, *as he seems to know,* those who are the reigning princes, reign by virtue of their personal merits.

It is the greatness of heart, the nobility of character, their superior qualities of observation, wisdom, love of Truth and Justice, that have raised them to the dignity of heirs to the thrones, of kings and queens. The crowns, by authority and the grace of God, have been thrown off, and they now rule by "the grace of divine humanity," chosen unanimously by recognition of their fitness to rule, and the reverential love of their voluntary subjects.

All around seems strangely changed. Ambition, grasping greediness or envy—miscalled Patriotism—exist no longer. Cruel selfishness has made room for just altruism and cold indifference to the wants of the millions no longer finds favour in the sight of the favoured few. Useless luxury, sham pretences—social and religious—all has disappeared. No more wars are possible, for the armies are abolished. Soldiers have turned into diligent, hard-working tillers of the ground, and the whole globe echoes his song in rapturous joy. Kingdoms and countries around him live like brothers. The great, the glorious hour has come at last! That which he hardly dared to hope and think about in the stillness of his long, suffering nights, is now realised. The great curse is taken off, and the world stands absolved and redeemed in its regeneration! . . .

Trembling with rapturous feelings, his heart overflowing with love and philanthropy, he rises to pour out a fiery speech that would become historic, when suddenly he finds his body gone, or, rather, it is replaced by another body . . . Yes, it is no longer the tall, noble Form with which he is familiar, but the body of somebody else, of whom he as yet knows nothing. . . . Something dark comes between him and a great dazzling light, and he sees the shadow of the face of a gigantic timepiece on the ethereal waves. On its ominous dial he reads:

NEW ERA: 970,995 YEARS SINCE THE INSTANTANE-OUS DESTRUCTION BY PNEUMO-DYNO-VRIL OF THE LAST 2,000,000 OF SOLDIERS IN THE FIELD, ON THE WESTERN PORTION OF THE GLOBE. 971,000 SOLAR YEARS SINCE THE SUBMERSION OF THE EU-ROPEAN CONTINENTS AND ISLES. SUCH ARE THE DECREE OF ORLOG AND THE ANSWER OF SKULD . . .

He makes a strong effort and—is himself again. Prompted by the Soul-Ego to *remember* and *act* in conformity, he lifts his arms to Heaven and swears in the face of all nature to preserve peace to the end of his days—in his own country, at least.

★★★★★★

A distant beating of drums and long cries of what he fancies in his dream are the rapturous thanksgivings, for the pledge just taken. An abrupt shock, loud clatter, and, as the eyes open, the Soul-Ego looks out through them in amazement. The heavy gaze meets the respectful and solemn face of the physician offering the usual draught. The train stops. He rises from his couch weaker and wearier than ever, to see around him endless lines of troops armed with a new and yet more murderous weapon of destruction—ready for the battlefield.